English Doesn't Suck

English Doesn't Suck

By

Alice Courtney and Sue Skidmore

Cover design by Kolby McLean

English Doesn't Suck is published by DABROADS 3, LLC, Phoenix, Arizona, 2010. For information, please correspond through *englishdoesntsuck.com.*

First Edition

ISBN 978-0-578-04748-5

Dedication

To Dave, Mark, Jean, and, of course, Desiree

Table of Contents

Introduction

There's no such thing as gravity; the whole world sucks!

Well, not quite. These things suck:

- Losing your hair and your waistline
- Vacuum cleaners
- Vampires
- Leeches
- Taxes
- Politicians
- SUVs
- Insurance companies
- The economy

Even our icon, Desiree, a pesky mosquito, sucks. Born into French aristocracy, Desiree lived a pampered childhood. When she morphed into an insect, she flew across the Atlantic and landed in Tombstone, Arizona. She became a regular at the Bird Cage Saloon where she did favors for the likes of Wyatt Urp and Doc Hadhisday. As her renown spread, so did the diseases she carried. In fact, Desiree is credited with snuffing out hundreds of mining camps across the Southwest. Her bravado, her reckless behavior, and her sordid proclivities were astounding. When we visited Desiree's resting place on Boot Hill, we were overcome. We knew we had to resurrect her for our book. Why? Her epitaph read:

Desiree lies here, the famous vamp
Who entertained from camp to camp.
The tricks she did were next to none
That broad knew how to have great fun.
Her life was filled with joy and bucks.
Desiree was the *queen of frontier sucks.*

Yes, these things suck, but **English doesn't suck!**

We Get It

Any person learning English will find it overwhelming. Imagine trying to decipher these sentences:

1. The psychologist had to subject the subject to a series of tests.
2. When I saw the tear in my dress, I shed a tear.
3. The Marine made a decision to desert his dessert in the desert.
4. A Polish family in my neighborhood liked to polish its cars on Saturday.
5. A dove dove into the underbrush.
6. The clothes were hung too close to the closet door, and I couldn't close it.
7. After he had read a book about the red tide, he stated, "It was a good read."
8. My invalid mother discovered her health insurance was invalid.
9. The buck does numerous antics when he sees a herd of does.
10. The gardener loved to produce produce.
11. The musician painted a bass on his bass horn.
12. At the present time, there is no one available to present the present to the winner.
13. As he was led from the cell, the prisoner was asked to lead the way to the spot where he had buried the lead pipe.
14. It was difficult to wind the kite string in the high wind.
15. He did object when he learned he was no longer the object of her affection.

If that isn't enough, consider this pronunciation nightmare:

Though we were thorough in our investigation, it was rough to determine if we were through. We thought we provided tough evidence, and our client decided there was no more dough to warrant further research. So until the proverbial bough breaks, we ought not worry. We will remain on the payroll of the public trough.

English is NOT easy, but don't worry. Desiree is here to suck the misery out of English. With her help and our guidance, you can do it.

Can't write well? Feel confused when asked to submit something in writing? Panic when having to send a memo to your boss or to an important client? So what if you cheated your way through English classes, or if you live in fear that you'll be discovered as an incompetent writer, this humorous reference guide can help you. It will help explain some basic writing rules, will offer opportunities to practice those long-forgotten skills and will build your confidence to approach any writing task.

WARNING: The stories and examples you are about to read are not about any real people or events. (Actually, yes, they are, but we did change their names to make it less likely that you would recognize them at the grocery store and point fingers.) If you are easily offended by caustic humor and ribald comments, you may want to purchase the 'family friendly' version of the guide.

SPECIAL BONUS GIFT

We've been told:

- Trust the government.
- If you do it once, you can't get pregnant.
- Daddy/Mommy knows best.
- Don't do that, or hair will grow in the palm of your hand.
- Young ladies never eat ice cream on dates, for it gives them pointees. (Catholic nun warning)

As times change, what was thought to be universally-valid truths change. For example, Columbus found that the world was not flat, Cherie did it once and did get pregnant, and Daddy invested his life savings in aluminum siding.

Our gift to you? Pithy bits of wisdom with which you can win friends and influence, well, no one. But we have found them to be… Absolute Truths.

Throughout our book, you will find absolute truths. They will be **bolded,** asterisked, and noted as ***(AT)**. Some examples follow for you to savor:

- **Diarrhea makes a mess.*(AT)** *(More on that later.)*
- **Liposuction sucks.*(AT)**
- **In a retirement community, no one cares that Tom served prison time for murdering his wife. The women know he's single and hope he can still drive at night.*(AT)**

If you find 100 ATs, email us, and we will send you a straw and a gift certificate to our favorite restaurant, Eat and Get Gas. If you find fewer, you're still a winner. (The straw really sucks.)

The Honkin' Big Eight

The Honkin' Big 8

Since most of us are not destined to compete on the flavor-of-the-day game show, we don't care how many parts of speech there are in English. But your writing is going to suck if you don't use these correctly.

1. **Noun**: name of a thing (You learned it as a person, place or thing; we just abbreviated it.)

    - When **Sue** and **Mark** traveled to **Colorado**, they met **Dick** and **Jane** at the **ranch**.
    - At the **campfire** that **night**, the **friends** celebrated by eating **steaks** and drinking **wine**.
    - **Sue** had too much **wine** to drink, woke up with a **headache,** and asked for **Alka-Seltzer®** and **aspirin**.
    - **Laughter** is the best **medicine** for a **person** with a **hangover**.

2. **Pronoun:** replaces the name of the thing

I	you	him	hers	our
me	your	his	it	ours
mine	yours	she	its	us
my	he	her	we	they
them	their	theirs		

- Jack always leaves **his** dirty underwear on the floor, and the cat makes **her** bed in **it.**
- **We** used to say that **our** marriage was heaven-made; then **we** got divorced.
- **It** is **your** turn to scrub the toilet; **my** turn was last week.

3. **Verb:** what things do

    - Jean **went** to the bar to meet her new boy on their first date.

- Her friend **was** late, but Jean **sat** quietly and **waited** patiently.
- When she **had remained** in the bar for more than 30 minutes, she **left** and **stomped** out angrily.
- She **remembered** that in college she **would wait** only 10 minutes for a professor to arrive, and then she **would leave** class.
- Her date **deserved** more time but not that much more.
- **Would** he **be** angry? Jean no longer **cared.**

You Suck Uh-Oh!

A *noun and/or pronoun + a verb = a sentence*. If you do not have those basic parts, you have committed a catastrophic mistake from here on referred to as a *You Suck Uh-Oh!*

The rest of the *Honkin' Big 8* add the color, emphasis, and interest to your writing. These help you *show* your reader instead of *tell* him. Using these means you've grown up and put on your 'big girl' panties!

4. Adjectives: describe things

- The **dirty, old** man leered at her **bodacious** tatas.
- He had experienced **wet** dreams before, but this one was more **vivid.**
- His skin was **clammy;** his heart was fluttering.
- The **unrelenting** thunderstorm of perspiration continued to saturate his **blue, satin** sheets.

Adjectives in comparison:

- Add **er** when comparing two things: The woman in the green dress is **hot,** but the one in the red dress is **hotter.**

- Add **est** when comparing three or more things: Of all the women at the bar, the one in the red dress is the **hottest.**

- With most adjectives that have two or more syllables, do not change the form of the adjectives. Instead, use the word **more** when comparing two things and **most** when comparing three or more things: Letterman is **more** entertaining than Leno, but Carson was the **most** entertaining of all.

- **NEVER use both an –er and more, or both an –est and most.** Incorrect example: *When she shaved her moustache, it was the **most happiest** day of her husband's life*. Correct Example: *When she shaved her moustache, it was the **happiest** day of her husband's life.*

5. **Adverbs:** describe how, when, where, and how much. Most, but not all, adverbs end in **-ly.**

    - Sue is **truly** sorry for forgetting to iron Mark's socks.

    - If you **suddenly** feel pain in your trigger finger, **immediately** stop playing the video game.

    - **Where** did I leave my tightie-whities? I am **really** worried that I left them under your dresser.

6. **Prepositions:** words that tell anywhere a prostitute goes, i.e. **on** the corner, **between** the sheets, **in** the limo, but never **at** the end **of** a sentence.

Behold the list of common prepositions--not to be confused with propositions.

above	about	across	along	among
around	at	before	behind	below
beside	between	by	down	during
except	for	from	in	inside

into	of	off	on	over
past	through	to	toward	under
up	upon	with	within	without

This isn't the entire list, just some of the most common. The full list numbers well over 50.

- **Around** 8:00 PM **in** a secluded part **of** the bar, Jean downed her third glass **of** merlot.

- The disc jockey **at** the front **of** the bar was playing blasts **from** her past.

- She gazed **across** the bar and spied her ex **among** the incoming patrons. **Beside** her lay her trusty gun. **Until** this moment, she did not think she was capable **of** murder.

- Her palms were sweaty; she reached **under** the table **for** her purse.

- Then, **without** further hesitation, Jean stood and moved **behind** his bar stool and paint-balled his designer shirt. **In** her mind, he was dead**.**

7. **Conjunctions: You can remember these as FANBOYS:** *F*or, *A*nd, *N*or, ***B**ut, **O**r*, *Y*et, ***S**o.* These link words, ideas, and sentences.

   - Allen slowly climbed the ladder rope up to the tree house, **for** he had been banished from the bedroom again.

   - Never think that blondes are dumb, **nor** underestimate their shrewdness.

   - She wanted to get liposuction, **yet** she was afraid of the risks **and** possible complications.

Either/or go together as do *neither, nor, never,* and *not.*

8. **Interjections:** (express strong feeling or surprise, such as

***whoopee, whoa, ouch, oh, hey, ah*)**

Often an interjection is a fragment, as in **Duh!,** that is followed by an exclamation point. While we would love to give you a complete list, we have discovered that interjections come and go as quickly as women's moods. Below, please find our best lists of interjections and the sentences they inhabit.

Old School Interjections

Alas	Egad	Eureka	Neato	Gadzooks
Alack	Eek	Golly Gee	Cool	Shazam

Common Interjections

Ah	Cool	Oh	Bravo	Hey
Aha	Darn	Ouch	Whoa	Wow

Current Interjections

Uh-oh	OMG	Holy $#@%	Duh	Tru dat
WTF	As if	Coolio	Sick	Bitchin'
Hello	Arrgh	Not	Gotcha	Fosho

Do you like to interrupt or be the center of attention in a conversation? Then use an interjection.

- ***Wow!*** I can't believe you stole that car.
- ***Ouch!*** These handcuffs really hurt.
- ***Arrgh!*** It's a pirate's life for me.

Mark It!

Mark It!

Punctuation signs are used to clarify meaning. Read the following:

Shes a self described computer butt nugget who would rather be surfing the Maui waves she hates to be alone with a computer its a nightmare

This is rat dung! Is Shes a name? Or did the writer mean She's (she is)? Does Shes like or hate waves? We will never know.

End Marks: those marks placed at the butt of your miraculous sentence

1. Period (.): a dot at the end of a sentence, not a monthly concern

- The dog went poo in the yard**.**
- Luckily, this happened in the neighbor's yard**.**
- I picked it up**.**
- But, that became a difficult chore because the flies were buzzing around it**.**

2. Exclamation point (!): after a word or a group of words that show strong emotion

- Wow**!** You really did well on that stupid grammar test.
- You came in at 3:00 AM. That's too late for a 12-year-old**!**
- Kudos to you**!** I can't imagine how you won that poker bracelet.
- Don't go there**!**

3. Question mark (?): at the end of a question

- Are you kidding me**?** Who cares**?**
- It's so late; are you really going bar hopping tonight**?**
- Do I really have to review for an eye exam**?**

Other less-famous marks that can be used anywhere

4. Comma (,): Most have heard or read about the Canadian company that almost lost over $2 million by omitting a comma that was vital to contractual language. Others may recall an elementary school lesson about missing commas, as in the following:

"Let's eat Tommy." Now, unless this was spoken by Alferd Packer, we suspect the writer meant: *"Let's eat, Tommy."*
There are SIX major uses of a comma.

A. **Words in a series:** Think of a grocery list or a 'To Do' list; then, instead of making the list, put them side by side with commas to separate the items.

- Momma is going to the grocery store for wine**,** lettuce**,** cereal**,** wine**,** toilet paper**,** coffee**,** bread**,** milk**,** wine**,** tampons**,** wine**,** and chicken. Momma is a wino.

- I saw London**,** I saw France**,** and I saw Collette's underpants.

Think of a number of adjectives to describe this actual event that occurred in Phoenix, Arizona, in July, 2009.

Here is our attempt:

> On a steaming, sultry, July day, Miss Calamity Bean opened the black, iron gate. While her checkered, weathered fly mask prevented her from estimating the depth of the water, she wandered into the clear, cool water. When her shoeless, frantic, hysterical owner called 911....

B. **Interrupters**: Place a comma ***before and after*** words that interrupt the flow of the sentence, not to be confused with lava.

- Jennifer Ruth, **Colorado's Attorney General,** announced her retirement today.
- I**, of course,** am a diva because I'm the youngest.

C. **FANBOYS (*For, And, Nor, But, Or, Yet, So*):** Place a comma between two complete thoughts connected with a FANBOYS.

- Arizona has a temperate climate in the winter**, but** its summers force the Devil to take an Alaskan cruise.
- Many consumers have been wary to spend money on nonessentials**, and** they have also cut back on charitable donations to Indian casinos.

D. **Introductory Material**: Place a comma after opening intro.

- **On behalf of my fellow senators,** I am pleased to announce the funding of the New York City to Paris bridge project.
- **Making his way through the crowded casino,** Dave finally reached the poker table.

E. **Everyday stuff that needs to be separated**
Place a comma between names and titles, dates, addresses, and numbers.

- **Title:** Mark Kolbe**, JD,** has opened a free legal clinic for sex addiction.
- **Date and Address:** The American Revolution began on April 19**,** 1775**,** when a group of colonists fired on the British at Lexington.
- **Address:** Her parents resided at 513 Elm Street**,** Youngstown**,** Ohio**,** until they moved to the poor house.
- **Numbers:** What are the chances that *English Doesn't Suck* will become a best seller: 1 in 1**,**000**,**000**,**000**,**000**,**000**,**000**,**000?

F. **Direct Quotations:** Use a comma and quotation marks to set off direct quotes.

- Mark Twain once said**,** **"**Fleas can be taught anything that a congressman can."
  "I never expected to see the day,**"** mused Will Rogers**,** **"**when girls get sunburned in the places they do."

5. Apostrophe ('): This is a comma under the influence. Yes, it's high. Use an apostrophe:

A. To show possession or ownership--singular words

- The boy**'s** stinky socks littered the locker room floor. (the socks belonging to the boy)
- Columbia University**'s** graduates face an uncertain job market.
  (the graduates of Columbia University)
- Jesus, Jose, and Maria**'s** mother volunteers at their school.
  (the mother of Jesus, Jose, and Maria--NOTE the apostrophe is placed on the last word in the group, not the others. If the three children had different mothers, it would be expressed: Jesus's, Jose's, and Maria's mothers volunteer at their school.)
- *For singular words ending in s:* The school bus**'s** emergency exit was blocked with band instruments.

B. To show possession or ownership--plural words. The apostrophe *follows after* the s.

- The boys**'** stinky athletic socks littered the locker room floor.
  (The socks belonging to the boys on the team)
- Across the country, most of the universities**'** graduates face an uncertain job market.
- **Teenagers' lives thrive on drama and their parents' credit cards.*(AT)**

C. To show contractions--the apostrophe replaces a missing letter or letters

I	+	am	=	I'm
You	+	are	=	You're
He/She	+	is	=	He's/She's
I	+	will	=	I'll
You	+	will	=	You'll
He/She	+	will	=	He'll/She'll
I	+	would/had	=	I'd
You	+	would/had	=	You'd
He/She	+	would/had	=	He'd/She'd
We	+	are	=	We're
They	+	are	=	They're
We	+	will	=	We'll
They	+	will	=	They'll
We	+	would/had	=	We'd
They	+	would/had	=	They'd
Let	+	us	=	Let's
Who	+	is/has	=	Who's

D. The vanishing not

Can	+	not	=	Can't
Should	+	not	=	Shouldn't
Could	+	not	=	Couldn't
Would	+	not	=	Wouldn't
Do	+	not	=	Don't
Does	+	not	=	Doesn't
Will	+	not	=	Won't
Was	+	not	=	Wasn't
Were	+	not	=	Weren't

You Suck Uh-Oh!

It (the neutered pronoun) Use an apostrophe if your intent is: it is or it has. **It's** been a great day at the bordello.

DO NOT use an apostrophe if the word 'it' possesses something.

The cat licked **its** paws.

Read your sentence out loud and substitute *it is* where you're thinking of putting *it's*. Nine times out of ten, you will hear the mistake and make the right choice!

Other confusing contractions:

- Your and you're
  Your = belonging to you
  You're= You are

  If **you're** going to charge the hotel room, enter **your** credit card number below.

- Whose and who's
  Whose = belonging to whom
  Who's = who is

  Who's scheduled to clean the bathroom today? **Whose** dirty underwear is on the floor?

- They're = they are

  They're going on vacation to Maui and plan to leave their children at home.

  When Alice and Dave get to Mexico, **they're** going to bestaying with Alice's cousins.

- Their = belong to them

They left **their** luggage in **their** car and walked to the hotel registration desk.

- There = not here

  The parking lot is over **there.**

6. Colon (:): two vertical dots on top of each other, and its use is never referred to as a colonoscopy.
There are four major uses of the colon:

A. Set off a formal list of items

- Before going to the mall, please complete the following chores**:** finish your homework, mow the lawn, feed the dogs, and clean your pig sty.
- Teachers often grade papers focusing on these**:** content, ideas, organization, voice, spelling and punctuation.

B. Introduction of a formal business letter

- Dear Sir**:**
- To whom it may concern**:**
- Hey Stupid**:**

C. Time

- We will meet at the Soiled Dove Tavern for drinks and appetizers at 3**:**30 PM on Thursday.
- You came in at what time? It was more like 3**:**00 AM. You're grounded!

D. Anatomy 101

- See your doctor for correct usage.

7. Semicolon (;): (half a colon) a comma with a dot on top of it; its use is never referred to as a sigmoidoscopy or a partial colonoscopy. We like to refer to it as a *'big-boy'* comma.

A semicolon is used to separate two, complete sentences. This punctuation mark is used in place of comma + a FANBOYS.

- Malcolm was arrested for drunk driving**;** he spent the night in jail.
- A well-known celebrity was arrested for drunk driving**;** he autographed several photos for the sheriff.
- The sheriff sold the autographs at an on-line auction site**;** he retired on his earnings.

8. Quotation Marks (" "): Quotation marks are two pair of drunken commas, flying high across the page. While some tweens adore using quotation marks to emphasize words, it is sick and wrong.

Use quotation marks to:

A. Signal a direct quotation

- **"** I'm really good at sex because I practice a lot alone," mused Woody Allen.

- According to Bruce Wallace, **"**My wife has doubled in size during our twenty years of marriage.**"** Then he added, **"**Wish I could say the same about my stock portfolio.**"**

- **"**Where did you get your hair cut?**"** asked Jack.

  "On my head,**"** she answered.

B. Quote no more than four lines of poetry or prose (For a research paper, consult style requirements.)

- **"**Out damn'd spot! Out, I say!**"** was spoken by Lady Macbeth, and she wasn't talking about lipstick on his collar.

- In her famous poem, she wrote, **"**Hickory, Dickory, Dock/ Two mice ran up the clock. The clock struck one/ and the other dropped dead of fright.**"**

C. Quote within a quote (This is tricky.) Single quotation marks are used to enclose a quotation within a quotation.

- "Young children quickly learn the adage of Benjamin Franklin, 'Mine is better than ours,' when it comes to sharing toys," posited psychologist, Anne Evans. (Evans is quoting Franklin.)

- "'Never answer a letter when you are angry' is an ancient Chinese proverb that one should remember before firing off an email to a crazy parent," said the principal. (The principal is quoting a proverb.)

Indirect quotations, or those that do not use exact words, require NO quotation marks, as in the following:

- She swears she's never had liposuction, but her spandex says otherwise.

- When the English professor asked his student why she had missed so many periods, she replied that she was menopausal.

9. Hyphen (-): This little, punctuation mark is so odd that we suggest you consult a dictionary because some words require hyphens, such as mother-in-law, while others like bridegroom, do not. **Before you marry your bridegroom, check out your potential mother-in-law first.* (AT)**

There are four uses of a hyphen:

A. Compound adjectives that describe a thing (noun)

- Frank is a **middle-aged** buffoon with a **six-pack-beer** gut.

- Sadie has been working **ten-hour** shifts at the massage parlor.

B. Numbers and fractions

- Remember **three-fourths** of the world's population has no access to a free, elementary education.

- In their **forty-five** years of marriage, Madge and Robert never had a fight. (They must be liars or on drugs.)

C. Some prefixes and some suffixes

- My **ex-husband** had the audacity to marry his best friend's **ex-wife**.
- The **president-elect** of the retirement association resigned when she was exposed as a silent partner in C. Us. Screwem, Inc.

The Seven Deadly Sins of Writing

The Seven Deadly Sins of Writing

First Sin (Laziness): *Writing hideous sentences*

1. Sentence design: In 'The Honkin' Big 8' chapter, we said that a sentence had to have a noun/pronoun plus a verb. We didn't mean you should stop there. Most of us don't talk in simple sentences: *Mosquitoes suck! That hurt. Kill it.* So don't write that way. Write like you talk; use a mixture of complex and/or compound sentences. Check these out; the noun/pronoun and verb are in bold.

- When Angelica was seventeen, her **mother** and **father sent** her to the convent.
- **Angelica had lived** the reckless, wanton life of a high school cheerleader and **was** not **pleased** to be sequestered among pious, old women.
- Why **am I forced** to live like this? **I am going** to escape.
- **Angelica fled** into the forest, and **she hid** in a remote cabin.
- **She knew** the nuns would come looking for her; **she was terrified** of the consequences.
- Of course, the **nuns** never **came.**
- **Angelica awoke** from her nightmare and **vowed** never to cheer and drink root beer again.

You Suck Uh-Oh!

2. Sentence Fragments: (or sentences that are missing a noun/ pronoun and/or a verb and don't express a complete thought.) To mend a fragment usually a word(s) must be added, appropriate punctuation inserted, or a dependent word deleted.

- You can't buy fireworks in this state. Regardless of your age.

Regardless of your age is a fragment.

CORRECT SENTENCE: You can't buy fireworks in this state, regardless of your age.

- If dentists did not use drills. *The entire group of words is a fragment.*

  CORRECT SENTENCE: If dentists didn't use drills, people would not dread their check-ups.

- He likes sports cars. Particularly Ferraris and Corvettes. *Particularly Ferraris and Corvettes* is a fragment.

  CORRECT SENTENCE: He likes sports cars, particularly Ferraris and Corvettes.

3. Diarrhea Sentences: Your sentence has the runs, also known as the 'Green Apple Squits.' It just runs on and on and on. Most English texts call these comma splices. It's easy to fix. Usually, it just needs the right punctuation.

- Dave broke his finger when the tennis racket slipped out of his hand the coach had warned him to tighten his grip he just didn't take her seriously. **(Really messy! Don't be lazy, clean it up!)**

  CORRECT SENTENCES: Dave broke his finger when the tennis racket slipped out of his hand. The coach had warned him to tighten his grip, but he just didn't take her seriously.

- Colter is eighteen-months-old and throws temper tantrums when he doesn't get his way his mother caters to his fits by picking him up kissing him and giving him cereal which stops his tantrum until he realizes that his mother is on the cell phone which gives him the opportunity to throw another fit stand in the corner take a dump in his diaper and toss yesterday's newspapers from the trash can. **(Can you smell the stink?)**

  CORRECT SENTENCES: Colter is eighteen-months-old

and throws temper tantrums when he doesn't get his way. His mother caters to his fits by picking him up, kissing him, and giving him cereal. This stops his tantrum until he realizes that his mother is on the phone. So he throws another fit, stands in the corner, takes a dump in his diaper, and tosses yesterday's newspaper from the trash can.

Second Sin (Anger): *Composing disagreeable sentences*

It can be really ugly when there's no agreement. When sentences don't have agreement, they are grotesque! Agreement issues to consider:

1. **Subject-verb Agreement:**
   singular subject + **singular verb** = agreement
   plural subject + **plural verbal** = agreement
   - The *stallion* **romps** across the meadow in search of a mare.
   - The *senators* **have returned** from caucus to announce their displeasure with campaign-spending limits.
   - Many *folks* at the baseball game **were booing** at the umpire.
   - The *music* blasting from his stereo **annoys** the neighborhood.
   - What **was** the *cause* of the botched facelift?
   - There **is** a *number* of reasons why this sentence is grammatically correct.

WATCH OUT! TRICKY SINGULAR PRONOUNS BELOW

- *Neither* of the boys confessed **his** guilt in stealing the condoms.
- If *everything* has **its** place, why can't I remember **its** place?

- *Everyone* dreads **his** or **her** colonoscopy exam. (If one chooses not to use *his* or *her*, the sentence could be written: Most *folks* dread **their** colonoscopy exams.)
- **Tricky singular pronouns take singular verbs!**

anyone	one	either	anybody
no one	each	neither	everybody
someone	anything	nothing	something
everyone	nobody	somebody	everything

- **Does** *anyone* **want** to be elected to a school board? *Everyone* **complains** that *everything* **is** wrong with public schools.
    - *Each* of the tomatoes **was inspected** by the border guard for contraband.
    - *Neither* Austin nor Paul **is performing** at the male burlesque show.
    - *Everybody* **loves** Grandma's stuffed cabbage rolls, but *nobody* **likes** the results of eating too many.

Two or more subjects joined with ***and*** require a plural verb.

- *Tom, Anne, **and** Nancy* **are going** to the school board meeting.
- **Taxes, health care, and insurance rates *need* to be overhauled.* (AT)**

2. **Pronouns and Antecedent Agreement:** Pronouns must agree in number and sex with the noun they replace—otherwise known as the antecedent.
    - **When the *senators* returned from caucus, they announced their displeasure with campaign-spending limits.* (AT)**
    - My *television* was not compatible with digital technology, and **it** needed to be replaced.

3. **Time Zone Agreement:** Many writers intermix verb tenses. They begin writing an email, essay, or letter using present-tense verbs and shift, sometimes mid-sentence, to past or future-tense verbs. Not only does this confuse the reader, but it screams, **"My writing sucks!"**

   Imagine receiving this email as a formidable supplier of building supplies:

   > Yesterday I was in a meeting and I overhear two guys talking about a project they work on. They were trashing a supplier they use on the project for providing inferior materials. City inspectors investigate and decide to sue the supplier. Thought you should know. I think it's your company.

   Although the writer used the past tense *was, were trashing, and thought,* the writer then changed to present tense *overhear, use, investigate, and decide.* As the reader, you've no idea whether this is a current project or a project that was completed years ago for which you may have already been investigated and held harmless.

   > When the **time** of the action actually changes from past, present, or future, shift the tense. Otherwise, keep it in the same time zone.

Third Sin (Greed): *Splitting hares, not infinitives*

An infinitive is a verb form used after the word **to.** For example, **to read, to drink, to frolic, to gamble**

Some writers "split" the infinitive by adding another word between **to** and the verb **read, drink, frolic, or gamble.** The following are examples of split infinitives:

- Megan wanted to quickly read her book report.
- Wally wanted to immediately drink his beer and to

simultaneously gamble at the slot machines.

This split causes English teachers, editors, and grammarians **to seize** the red pen and **to scribble** scathing comments about how much the writer sucks!

The correct forms of these examples are:

- Megan wanted to read her book report quickly.
- Wally wanted to drink his beer and to gamble simultaneously.

Fourth Sin (Lust): *Dangling your participles or misplacing your modifiers*

1. **Dangling Participles:** A participle is a verb, but in this case it acts like an adjective by describing a noun.

   The woman **standing** there is my husband's girlfriend.
   Standing is used to describe my husband's girlfriend.

Dangling a participle is similar to neglecting to wear an athletic supporter. Look these over, and you will understand.

- Quietly munching hay, I watched the stallion in the pasture. *(Was I munching hay? I don't think so. The stallion was.)*

  Correct Sentence: I watched the stallion in the pasture quietly munching hay.

- While fiddling on the fiddle, Rome burned. *(Oh, really? Rome is a violinist?)*

  Correct Sentence: While Nero fiddled the fiddle, Rome burned.

2. **Misplaced Modifiers:** Simply put, a misplaced modifier is placing a word(s) in the wrong place at the wrong time. This is similar to meeting your probation officer as you exit the gun and munitions shop.

- I bought a car from a used car dealer with a leaky radiator. *(Excuse me. Does the dealer have a leaky radiator? If so, he needs Depends®.)*

  Correct Sentence: The car I bought from the used car dealer had a leaky radiator.

- She put the sandwiches back in the bag she had not eaten. *(Wow! She must have been really full not to have eaten the bag.)*

  Correct Sentence: She put the sandwiches she had not eaten in the bag.

- At the age of six, my family moved to Ohio. *(That's a feat for the record books.)*

  Correct Sentence: When I was six-years-old, my family moved to Ohio.

Fifth Sin (Envy): *Coveting unbalanced sentences*

Libras like balance, banks like balance, and tightrope walkers like balance. English teachers like balanced writing. When sentences are awkward and unbalanced, they contain faulty parallelism. Equal ideas must be expressed in equal form.

- The gigolo likes fancy restaurants, loose women, and sports cars made in Italy.

  Correct Sentence: The gigolo likes fancy restaurants, loose women, and Italian sports cars.

- During our vacation in Vietnam, we drank duck blood, ate something that resembled dog, and had the green-apple squits.

  Correct Sentence: During our vacation in Vietnam, we drank duck blood, ate dog meat, and had the green-apple squits.

- You can get to Mexico by car, bus, or fly.

Correct Sentence: You can get to Mexico by car, by bus, or by plane.

- My son's fraternity house was filthy, disgusting, and reeked of vomit.

Correct Sentence: My son's fraternity house was filthy, disgusting and smelly.

Sixth Sin (Gluttony): *Eliminating obesity in writing and refraining from drinking the whole bottle at one sitting*

Many writers think that the use of copious amounts of words (aka **deadwood)** makes them sound smarter. It doesn't. KISS someone instead. (**K**eep **I**t **S**imple **S**tupid!)

AVOID	USE
at all times	always
at the present time	now
due to the fact that	as, since, because
in view of the fact that	as, since, because
in as much as	since
in the amount of	for
in the mean time	meanwhile
in the near future	soon
in the neighborhood of	nearly, about, around
in this place	here

previous to	before
there can be no doubt	doubtless
in reference to/or with regard to	about
rarely ever	rarely

Seventh Sin (Pride): *Being a doofus*

These are the most common errors that make you look like a doofus and will prevent you from advancing into the world of respected communication.

1. **Using contractions in formal writing**: In research papers, essays, and other formal documents use: cannot, it is, are not, they are, etc.

2. **Using the word "you" in formal writing:** As much as nursing is about administering medications and thorough patient assessments, it is also about the caring of the holistic patient; through meeting his/her physical, psychological, and spiritual needs. Most patients never remember the medications **you** gave them to save their lives, or **you** catching the early signs of a potentially-life threatening disease. They remember that **you** took the time to explain what was going on, made them feel safe, gave them a warm blanket, and held their hands when things got scary. *(Note the use of you in this college essay. The reader is saying, not me. I did not do those things. "You" antagonizes the reader.)*

3. **There = not here** (The parking lot is over *there*.) In formal writing it is best to avoid sentences that begin with there.

   - **There** are many people that believe English is a difficult language to master.

- **Simplify it:** Many people believe that English is a difficult language to master.

4. **Using multiple punctuation marks (???) or (!!!)** The multiple use of punctuation marks is for tweens and drama queens. One per customer please.

5. **Misusing *bring* and *take*** Use bring when something is moved from far to near. Use take when something is moved from near to far.
   - Daddy **brings** home the bacon; Mommy **takes** his dirty laundry to the cleaners.

6. **Using *then* for *than* or vice versa**
   - Then refers to a sequence of events: I went to the gym, and **then** I went to get an ice cream cone.

   - Than is used in comparisons: Men's colds are worse **than** women's colds.

7. **Misusing *lay* and *lie***
   - Use lay if someone is placing something somewhere: Momma **lays** her flyswatter on the counter. Momma **laid** her flyswatter on the counter. Momma **had laid** her flyswatter on the counter.

   - Use lie if someone or something is reclining: Momma **lies** in her bed until noon. Yesterday, Momma **lay** in her bed until noon. Momma **has lain** in her bed all week.

8. **Misusing *loose* (rhymes with goose) and *lose* (rhymes with shoes)**
   - Use loose if something is free or not tight: Anyone who has ever been around a goose knows the goose has **loose** bowels.

   - Use lose as a verb that means not win or misplace: My mother-in-law **loses** her money at the horse races.

9. **Misusing *good* and *well*** (Confusion arises because well can serve as an adjective meaning "good physical health" and as an

adverb.)

- Now that the fever has broken, I feel **well** again.
- He plays the trumpet **well**.
- I look **good** in blue.
- I'm feeling **good** about the math test. (Good refers to an emotional state, not physical state of health)

10. Misusing *bad* and *badly*

- I feel **bad** for the Arizona State Sun Devils. (The adjective bad describes the speaker's emotional health.)
- Their team played **badly**. (The adverb badly describes how the team played.)

But wait… there's more!

Unfortunately, English is filled with words that easily confuse all of us. These words are pronounced the same or nearly the same, but are **spelled** differently and have different **meanings**. Many word processing programs do not identify these errors in meaning when the word is spelled correctly. Imagine receiving the following emails:

- *Are company would like to bid on the project, and we offer the following preposition and advise.*

- *Far two many men have prostrate problems.*

- *Since I past the bar exam, I'd like to apply for a position in you're company rather then work for my father's firm.*

As a special bonus, we have included an extended list of words that confuse, bewilder or otherwise befuddle writers and their readers.

- **accept** *to admit or receive*
  except *exclude, excuse, or leave out*

  I have learned to **accept** all of my husband's proclivities, **except** his snoring.

- **adapt** *to change or alter*
  adopt *to take or bring in*

  Ashley has **adapted** to her life in North Carolina, but she has yet to **adopt** the Southern ya'll dialect.

- **advice** *something your Momma gives you*
  advise *to give guidance*

  Momma **advised** me to never have unprotected sex, but I never listened to her **advice**.

- **affect** *to cause something to change*
  effect *the result of the change*

  The **effects** of having unprotected sex greatly **affected** Dave's relationship with his Momma.

- **are** *a verb form of to be*
  our *belonging to us*

  Our Momma swats mosquitoes on our patio, and we **are** going to get her a new swatter for Christmas.

- **beggar** *a person who asks for money, not to be confused with a college alumni foundation*
  booger *a nasal substance that can be used as a snack or tossed at unsuspecting victims*
  bugger *a bad person*
  burger *a shortened form of hamburger until the inventions of veggie, tofu, gelatin, and chicken burgers*

  As I waited outside the **burger** joint, a **beggar** approached me and asked for money. Since I'm not a **bugger**, I gave him a dollar and some change. After he shuffled away, my luncheon date had yet to appear. I returned to my car, pulled down the visor mirror, checked my mascara, and surreptitiously searched my nasal cavities for **boogers**.

- **BoSox** *a Beantown baseball team*

Botox *a drug injected under one's skin to rid the said injection site of wrinkles*

While her boy toy was at the **BoSox** game, Ashley scheduled an appointment for **Botox**.

- **brake** *to slow down or stop or the thing that makes something slow down or stop*
  break *to destroy something or the thing that makes one rest*

  Meredith hit the **brakes** on her bicycle. She knew she'd **break** her ankle if she fell. With luck, she **braked** in time. After such an experience, she decided to take a **break**. She got off the wicked bike, grabbed her water bottle, and drank the Long Island Iced Tea.

- **but** *except or to the contrary.* ***But always follows the positive comments about your child's performance/behavior in a parent-teacher conference.*(AT)***
  butt *the end or one's posterior*

  I had been on the plane for three hours, and my **butt** was aching. I needed to stretch, **but** the captain had not turned off the "Fasten Seat Belt" sign.

- **canvas** *weird material that is used in tents and such*
  canvass *acts of soliciting, collecting and surveying the opinions of the public*

  The artist's **canvas** depicted several nude figures **canvassing** their neighborhood for signatures to permit Sunday sales of liquor.

- **capital** *the city that is home to state or federal government, first, or chief*
  capitol *the building housing state or federal government*

  The **capitol** dome at Boise, Idaho's state **capital**, has the state motto engraved in **capital** letters.

- **counsel** *to give advice or the person giving advice, e.g. your shrink*
  council *a group of folk that guide a club, planning commission, government*

  The City **Council's** attorney **counseled** the defendants that the proposed rezoning for the strip club would be an arduous battle.

- **elicit** *to bring out*
  illicit *improper or yucky*

  Kolby **elicited** the opinions of all of her constituents concerning the marketing of **illicit** sex on the streets of Las Vegas.

- **hear** *to audibly be informed*
  here *in this place, not there*

  We're **here** at the box office waiting to **hear** if we still have reservations for the midnight showing of *DaBroads Do Dallas.*

- **hole** *a cavity*
  whole *entire*

  She stuffed the **whole** package of dynamite down the gopher **hole**. Calmly, she lit the fuse and waited for those dastards to be blown to bits.

- **meet** *to encounter*
  meat *edible animal carcass*

  When cannibals **meet** new explorers, they are overwhelmed with the prospect of fresh **meat**.

- **passed** *completed, handed off, went by*
  past *not now*

  In **past** history, prostitutes were called soiled doves. These ladies never **passed** tests for syphilis; thus the venereal disease was **passed** from miner to miner.

- **pedal** *a mechanism that uses a foot*
  peddle *to sell*

  Seth stepped on the gas **pedal** and sped to the swap meet. He couldn't wait to **peddle** his cure for erectile dysfunction.

- **pore** *to study closely or the holes in one's skin*
  poor *substandard*
  pour *to flow freely*

  The sweat **poured** from the **pores** in his forehead. He'd spent the night **poring** over the divorce settlement and knew he was about to be a very **poor** man with a very high-priced girlfriend.

- **principal** *balance on a debt, head poobah of a school, or chief*
  principle *a rule, law, or truth*

  Our high school **principal**, Mr. Arnholt, announced that all students would follow the **principles** of courtesy at football games.

- **prostate** *a male gland*
  prostrate *lying down*

  After Paul's **prostate** surgery, he was **prostrate** for several hours.

- **road** *a dirt, gravel, or paved path used by pedestrians or vehicles*
  rode *yesterday's ride in or on a vehicle*
  rowed *yesterday's movement in an oar boat*

  Bruce **rode** his motorcycle down the country **road**. When he reached Campbell Lake, he parked the cycle, got in a dinghy, and **rowed** to the opposite shore.

- **role** *an actor or player's part*
  roll *a fancy piece of dough, to toss and turn, to beat a drum, to maneuver a plane in such a despicable fashion that one dirties his or her shorts*

  Each of the employees was awarded a bonus for his or her **role** in making the company a success. After a drum **roll**, each of the employee's names was announced and applauded.

- **seamen** *guys who like water, boats, and ships*
  semen *something to do with males*

  Sorry, we couldn't think of a great sentence. Use your imagination.

- **than** *a comparison word*
  then *relating to that time*

  When Paco discovered he was smarter **than** Isabella, he decided to steal her family jewels. **Then** he plotted to commit the crime.

- **to** *toward or before a verb as to testify*
  too *also or excess amount*
  two *the number 2*

  For **two** years, he spent far **too** many hours playing video games, and he had **to** have carpal tunnel surgery.

- **trader** *a person who exchanges one thing for another*
  traitor *a bad person who betrays his wife, girlfriend, or country*

  Clark was a well-known fur **trader** among many Native American tribes. His buddy, Lewis, was tried as a **traitor** and hanged in the public square.

- **wear** *to be clothed, to erode, or clothing*
  where *in what place*

“**Where** is the underwear department,” inquired Jack. “My boxers are showing signs of **wear**, and I need a new pair to **wear** to the wedding.”

- **weather** *climate conditions*
  whether *if*

  Whether they go to the Bahamas will depend on the **weather** advisory issued for Hurricane Harriet.

PWR

PWR

Before you paid good money to Vanna for a vowel, you'd have guessed this word. Yep, **power.** To become a better writer, you need to use **PWR (Prewriting, Writing, and Revising.)**

Prewriting

Prewriting includes finding a topic, drafting a topic sentence or thesis statement, and organizing ideas. Simply put: **Never write before you think.**

1. The topic
   - Sometimes you are assigned a topic about which to write.
   - However, if you have to come up with your own idea, write about what you know. If you've never swam naked in the ocean, don't write about it. If you and your thirteen-year-old friends stole the family car and went for a ride, that's a worthy story.
   - The best ideas come from brainstorming, doodling, making a list, or free writing.

Doodling an Idea

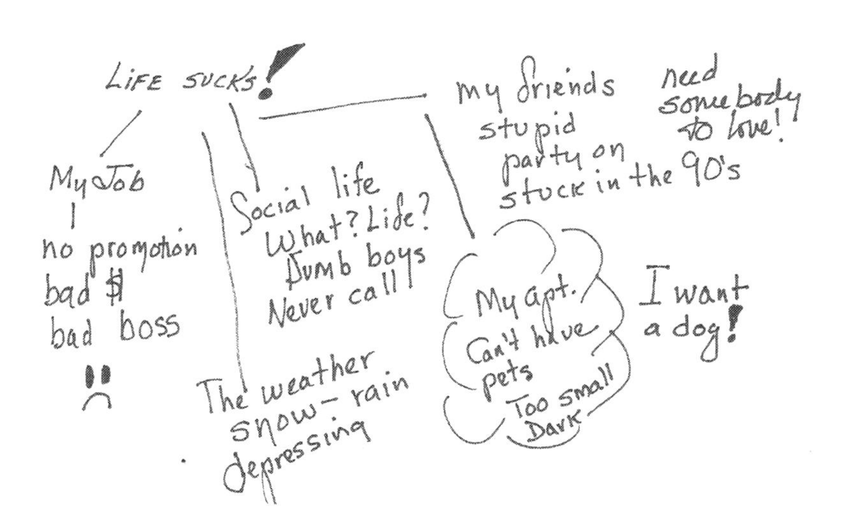

If you're writing a paper comparing and contrasting men's and women's colds, a list may be helpful.

Making a List

Colds

Men's Colds	Women's Colds
Can't get out of bed	Must get out of bed to tend to children, pets, and routine housework
Can't go to work	Must go to work to make the monthly mortgage payment
Behave like an ill child	Can't behave like a child--has to suck it up and work
No one has ever had such a bad cold.	It's just the sniffles.

2. After doodling or making a list, draft one sentence that contains your idea or **precise opinion** about the topic. This sentence is called a **topic sentence** for a paragraph or a **thesis statement** for an essay or research paper. Though the doodler had lots of thoughts, she wrote: *Dogs are great companions for single women.* The lister wrote: *Men's colds are worse than women's colds.*

Writing

Now that you have your topic sentence or thesis statement, you've conquered the second level of *English Doesn't Suck* and still have lifelines. We know you're afraid you'll fall off the cliff, crash, and burn. Hold our hands as we lead you through the strategies and breeds of writing.

It is easier to outline your thoughts before writing by using a simple format like the one below:

Topic Sentence/Thesis Statement: <u>Dogs are great companions for single women.</u>

Supporting Evidence 1: Companionship

Details: Love me when no one else does

Supporting Evidence 2: Improve my social life

Details: Won't have to go out with stupid friends

No more dumb boys

Supporting Evidence 3: Little dogs bring happiness

Details: Don't care about pee

Closing/conclusion: Dogs are single women's best friends.

There are two common ways to organize your evidence: chronologically or emphatically.

- Chronological order is organization based on time, e.g. what happened first, second? what to do first, next, last?
- Emphatic order is arranged least to most important/most convincing evidence, e.g. a certain habit should stop because it's socially unacceptable, it makes a mess, and it can cause blindness. NOTE: **Always save the best reason for last, for that's what the reader will remember.**

After completing her outline and considering organization, Bitsy wrote her first draft.

Dogs and Me

by Bitsy Blondell

Dogs are great companions for single women. How do I know that? My life sucks! If I had a dog, I'd have companionship. Dogs are friends. My dog would love me. Even though my boss hates me and will not promote me. My dog would replace my friends. My friends party too much and releve their high school days. Not to mention all those dumb boys that ask me out once and never call again!! If I had a dog, I would be sooo happy. Just a little dog. I wouldn't even mind cleaning up pee on the carpet. Dogs are single women's best friends. If I can't get a dog, I'll get a kitten.

Gag us with a spoon, Bitsy. This is an awful piece of writing. It sucks! If you think it is great, see the revising section immediately.

Writing Breeds

Calm down. This has nothing to do with mixing genes. There is a multitude of writing types from emails to research papers. Just like dogs, there are similarities and differences in each breed. Now that you have conquered prewriting, outlining, and organizing, suck it up. Fasten your seat belt. We're moving on to our most popular breeds.

1. Paragraph
2. Business Communications: including emails and letters
3. Essay
4. Research Paper

Paragraph

A paragraph is a related group of sentences that discuss ***one*** idea.

How to write a paragraph

1. **Topic sentence.** This is usually the first sentence of the paragraph.
2. **Evidence.** Use examples and details to explain and to convince the reader that your opinion is valid.
3. **Closing sentence.** This sentence brings finality to the paragraph.

Using the same format found in the appendix:

Topic Sentence: <u>Working in a bordello was my worst job.</u>

Supporting Evidence 1: grueling hours

Details: 60 hours a week, no weekends or holidays off

Supporting Evidence 2: lousy pay, minimal benefits

Details: $25 per hour, few tips, no health insurance

Supporting Evidence 3: demented clientele

Details: poor hygiene, bravado, weird expectations

Closing sentence: After spending three years at Miss Kitty's Parlor, I vowed to never prostitute myself again.

Paragraph example

Working in a bordello was my worst job. While I was going to college, I signed on to work at Miss Kitty's, where patrons come first. I thought the hours would allow me time to study, but I was wrong. I found myself working 60 hours a week, and I had no weekends or holidays off. Even on Christmas Day, Miss Kitty's Parlor had clients scheduled every half hour. Not only were the hours bad, but the wages and benefits were lousy. I made $25 an hour, but I was required to have my hair done and my body waxed weekly. By the time I deducted those expenses, I was taking home about $12 an hour and $20 in nightly tips. I received no benefits, such as sick leave nor insurances. Since Miss Kitty's was not exactly a legitimate business, the owner was not bound by federal employment regulation standards. Thus, I spent serious cash for infectious disease inoculations, salves, and ointments. However, the worst part of my job was dealing with demented clientele. Most of them suffered from poor hygiene; they reeked of alcohol and cigars. Many didn't shave or bother to brush the steak dinner out of their teeth. They would boast and brag about their sexual encounters, but when the time came, they couldn't. Further, kinky requests abounded. One of my clients paid me to apply blush, with a make-up brush, to his lily-white feet. Another asked me to recite nursery rhymes while he sat naked in a rocking chair. Finally the long hours, bad pay, and weird clients were unbearable, and I quit. After spending three years at Miss Kitty's Parlor, I vowed to never prostitute myself again.

Business Communications

Unless you have inherited Great Aunt Lucy's fortune, you **must master** this section. Without skills in business writing, you will spend your miserable life begging Mother Hubbard for a promotion.

Email

Mosquito bites kill; email kills. A poorly-written email can be as fatal to a contract, a business transaction, or a career, as malaria is to a third world country.

How to write an email

1. **Think.** Email is deadly because it's **immediate, public, and permanent**. In an instant, you can reply to an inquiry, ask a question, or break off a relationship; within seconds, you can receive a response. Your message can be forwarded to thousands across the network world. Even the sheik of a remote kingdom will know you are stupid! Thus, it is **critical** that you think before you write.

2. **Draft.** Yes, your computer, cell phone, or other electronic device will allow you to write a draft of your response to an angry customer or your boss. The draft should contain brief, logical sentences or bullet points that use professional business terms. A professional response *does not include*: BTW, OMG, WTF, :) or :(.

3. **Wait.** After at least 15 minutes have passed, open your draft and reread. Does your communication make sense? Have you used the right words, have you asked logical questions, have you proposed viable solutions? Are dates, times, monetary amounts correct? If you are satisfied, run spell check.

4. **Send.** Once you hit send, it's gone. If you made an error, it could be lethal. You may be shoveling dog doo for his Highness.

Email Example

Dr. Skidmore:

On behalf of the Society of Old Broads (SOB), I extend an invitation for you to participate in our July 12, 2010, training meeting.

We offer you:

- consultation fee of $2.99 per day
- lodging at the Beefcake Inn
- meals at the local senior center
- transfers to and from the Bubba County Airport

Please let me know if you can join us for this very important event.

Thank you,

Byrd Jae Onion, Executive Director

Society of Old Broads

Letters

Even in this hi-tech world, business letters are used both personally and professionally. Your job may demand that you initiate communication or respond to clients. At home, you may need to confirm a telephone conversation or send a letter of complaint. Though this breed of writing requires less time-sensitive action, it still demands rational thinking.

How to write business letters

1. **Draft a single sentence that states the purpose of the letter.**

    - After five years of temporary employment in your bordello, please consider my enclosed application for the full-time position of assistant madam.

    - I have received and reviewed your request to raise the limit on your credit card from $125 to $2,500.

2. **Draft the supporting details.** Dates, facts, evidence, and/or examples

3. **Follow stodgy format rules.** (Grow up! Every once in a while it is necessary to play by the rules.)

    - Heading includes your address and date. No, you don't rewrite the address if you're using the company letterhead.

    - Inside address is the name and address of the people you're writing.

    - Greeting: Dear Mrs. Masangil, Dear Sir, To whom it may concern, followed by a colon (:)

    - Body of letter arranged in paragraph form

    - Closing: Sincerely, Respectfully yours, Yours truly.

    - Your signature is followed by your typewritten name below.

Business Letter Example

1004 North Crenshaw
Durham, Ohio
December 29, 2009

Build You Up
1210 N. Madison
New York, New York 10230

Dear Sir or Madam:

I purchased your miracle, build-up bra for my wife for Christmas, and it came with a full, money-back guarantee if not completely satisfied. I am returning it because I am not satisfied. When I view my wife from the side, I cannot tell whether she is walking forward or backward. In other words, she does not have the appearance of gigantic mammary glands you promised!

My wife has suffered embarrassment for her small rack her entire life. Once she ripped open her blouse, bared herself to a lingerie department clerk, and asked for help. The clerk informed her that acne medicine was not sold in this store. My wife has tried elixirs, salves, and pills, none of which have grown her breasts. Your company's promise just seemed to be the miracle for which we had been hoping. Your bra didn't deliver. Please return my money.

Thank you for your attention to this matter.

Sincerely,

I. M. Hung, Senior

The Essay

Essay? Yes, essay. We know that word has caused you to dirty your boxers. Go change your undies, pour yourself a drink, and read on. Essays have less-threatening aliases. They are known as papers, reports, stories, and articles. An essay is nothing more than a bunch of paragraphs that relate to **one** topic.

Essays contain three parts:

- Introduction, or the **first** paragraph, gets the reader interested. It contains the thesis statement.

- Body, or a minimum of **three** paragraphs, provides evidence and examples. Each of these paragraphs has one topic sentences that discusses only one topic. (The size of this section can vary.)

- Conclusion, or **last** paragraph, summarizes and restates the thesis. This paragraph does **NOT** include any new information that was not previously discussed in the body.

Essay Outline

Introduction and Thesis Statement: <u>Class reunions are difficult to define, but the fortieth reunion is distinctive.</u>

Body Paragraph 1

Topic Sentence: The fortieth-year reunion is a must-attend event for it is a celebration of life.

Supporting Evidence:

Details: In memoriam, Joan, others, we made it to 40.

Body Paragraph 2

Topic Sentence: Secondly, there is a dearth of braggarts at the fortieth.

Supporting Evidence:

Details: millions, non-millions, arm candy, now old and fat

Body Paragraph 3

Topic Sentence: Finally, the fortieth solidifies the need for a forty-fifth.

Supporting Evidence:

Details: Too many dead, old, sick, moved away

Conclusion and restatement of the thesis: The fortieth-year class reunion is very different.

Essay Example

The Class Reunion

by Betty Fuchs

The invitation read, "Plan to attend the fortieth reunion of Chaney High School, Class of 1966 graduates." I reread the invitation. Yes, it said forty years. Where had forty years gone? Since the reunion was less than six weeks away, I had to get busy. I needed to lose fifty pounds, have eyelid surgery, get a visible tattoo, visit a trendy hair stylist, and buy a clingy outfit. I had to look my best. After all, it had been forty years. Class reunions are difficult to define, but the fortieth-year reunion is distinctive.

The fortieth-year reunion is a must-attend event, for it is a celebration of life. Most attendees are saddened to see the *In Memoriam* section of the video presentation, since their recollections of Joan were her coronation as homecoming queen, not as a murder victim. As another thirty or so names scroll across the screen, they remember soldiers of the Vietnam War and AIDS victims, and those lost to illnesses and accidents. When the video concludes, the alums congratulate each other for "making it to 40."

Secondly, there is a dearth of braggarts at the fortieth. Those who haven't made a million bucks aren't going to, those who have made a million no longer care, and those who formally travelled with gorgeous, arm-candy escorts are now bald, obese, or infirmed. This lack of one-up-man-ship garbage makes the event much more exhilarating. Conversations among attendees focus on real issues, such as grandchildren, erectile dysfunction, social security, and surgeries.

Finally, the fortieth solidifies the need for a forty-fifth. Everyone agrees that the ten-year cycle must change. Too many additional names will be listed on *In Memoriam* at the fiftieth. Too many alums will be strapped to a wheelchair, sentenced to a skilled-nursing facility, or ensconced in a double-wide mobile home in Florida to come to the fiftieth. A forty-five-year class reunion is a must!

The fortieth-year, class reunion is very different. Attendees celebrate their success for being alive, and the braggarts have ceased spinning tales. Further, the fortieth reunion reaffirms that life is too short to wait ten years for another party.

Essay Styles

Before writing an essay, the author must answer the question: What is its **purpose**? There are six common methods or arrangements of essays.

1. **Narration:** tells a story
    - An example might be: The day I got divorced was the happiest day of my life.
    - Organized chronologically

2. **Argumentation/Persuasion:** to convince or to persuade to a particular point of view or to strengthen or to change the opinion of the reader. It is not a fanatical, unreasonable approach.
    - Topic must be controversial enough to have a difference of opinion.
    - Organized emphatically—Save the BEST argument for last

3. **Compare/Contrast:** an examination of two or more things in order to establish similarities or differences. An analogy is an extended comparison: My life is a roller coaster.

4. **Cause/Effect:** a cause is a force, action, or influence that produces an effect. It it is the reason something happens. An effect is the result or product of a cause. It is whatever happens or what will happen if.
    - Organized emphatically
    - When writing about the cause and effect relationship, the writer can reason in several ways—causes and effects of WWII, or effect to cause (Why did it happen?), or cause to effect (What will happen if the bond issue doesn't pass? What

are the effects of dropping out of school?)

5. **Process:** a series of actions, changes, functions, steps, or operations that bring about a particular end or result.
    - Informational (How does it happen? How does it work? An example might be: How a body is embalmed or an explanation of an Amish wedding ceremony.)
    - Instructional (How do I do it? An example might be: How to make Grandma's stuffed cabbage rolls.)
    - Organized chronologically (What happens first, second, third.)

6. **Description:** specific details to create a clear picture of something or someone
    - Usually organized spatially—top to bottom, left to right, far to near

A detailed description of each of these modes follows on the next pages. Suck it up. Turn the page.

Narrative Paper

A narrative paper tells or recounts a story and is arranged chronologically. The paper answers: who, what, when, where, why, and how.

How to write a Narrative

1. **Think** of an-**est** experience--something that stirred strong feelings and created a lasting meaning: scari**est**, happi**est**, sadd**est,** sick**est,** funni**est,** **most** embarrassing.

2. Now if your happi**est** **experience** was a two-week vacation in Hawaii, narrow your topic. No one wants to read a day-by-day account of your trip, just as no one wants to sit through a four-hour slide show of your pictures. **Draft** a topic sentence, such as: *To climb Diamondhead is an exhilarating experience.*

3. **Determine point of view**. Will the paper be written from the first person perspective or "I"? Or from the third person perspective, "he/she/they."

    - "I" narratives are limited to the actions and events seen through the eyes of **one** person.

    - "He/she/they" narratives are omniscient, like someone perched high above the action watching and recording. These narratives allow the writer to portray events from various angles and reveal the thoughts and actions of all.

4. **Use vivid verbs and rich language** to carry the story, such as wobble, stagger, smack, crash, loiter, grumbled, stammered.

5. **Use rich dialogue** to reveal emotion and personality--not he said/ she said, but words such as, yelled, screamed, growled, answered, whispered, stated, stammered, responded, cried. **Remember to start a new paragraph each time the speaker changes.**

6. **Write a conclusion that brings closure to the story**. This is **NOT** a "to be continued" soap opera, and "the end" is not an appropriate conclusion.

Narrative Paper

My Visit to the Doctor

by Ashy Breathminton

I had done it all. I had endured my children's and husband's admonishments. I had been to re-hab, chewed copious amounts of nicotine gum, worn patches that defaced my skin, drank snake-oil elixirs; yet, nothing had worked. Tobacco consumed my soul.

Of course, I knew the consequences: lung cancer, emphysema, stroke, heart attack, and dastardly wrinkles. But the moment I awoke in the morning, all I wanted was a cigarette. The dreadful taste was exhilarating. However, by late afternoon, the taste became overwhelmingly delightful, especially when accompanied by a sip of cold beer.

Finally, I decided to consult a smoking therapist, Dr. Durham Bullarnholt. Dr. Bullarnholt asked me a series of questions to better understand my addiction. I answered "yes" to most. "When you wake do you have the urge to smoke? When you drink coffee or sweet tea do you want a cigarette?"

His probing continued for another half hour. "When you're at the casino, do you smoke? When you're anxious or upset do you smoke?"

Then, Dr. Bullarnholt dropped the bomb. "Do you smoke after intercourse?"

WTF kind of question was that? That caught me by surprise. After several moments I replied, "I don't know. I never looked."

Argumentation or Persuasion Paper

We don't lie. This is a **very** difficult paper to write because its purpose is to convince the reader that your position is valid or to change his attitude about a controversial issue. The writer must be definitive and passionate, without being disrespectful, and the writer cannot be fanatical nor unreasonable. Unlike much of life, this paper calls for sanity, facts, and logical thinking.

How to write Argumentation

1. Determine a debatable point, which is one that can't be proved or disproved by fact.

- Debatable points must be clear, not vague nor wishy-washy, such as *Sometimes marijuana should be legalized, and sometimes it shouldn't.* (The reader has no idea which side you support.)
- Bad debatable points: *Skiing is fun. I love oatmeal. Women live longer than men (statement of fact that is not debatable.)*
- Good debatable points: *Illegal immigration should be enforced. High schools place too much emphasis on competition.*

2. Determine the opposing arguments, for the proverb is correct: *There are two sides to every story.* The opposition should be acknowledged.

3. Gather convincing evidence, such as facts, statistics, verifiable evidence, and examples.

4. Organize evidence from least to most important evidence. Save the most compelling argument for last, for that's the one the reader will remember.

5. Draft paper using the pronouns he/she/one/they.

You Suck Uh-Oh!

Never use "you" in formal writing. Avoid using "I" because the focus should be on the topic, not the writer.

6. Draft a conclusion.

Persuasion Paper

Do You Swear?

by Georgia Washington Smith

Tell the truth. Swear to tell the truth. Always be truthful. Most of us were raised according to these adages. We learned the importance of truth at home, at church, and at school. As we grew older and senility set in, many of us adopted Mark Twain's advice, "If you tell the truth, you don't have to remember anything." While most of us agree that truth is a virtue, anyone who denies ever telling a lie is a liar. Often times lying is the best option.

Lying is acceptable when the truth would be devastating. In preparation for the charity ball, my mother spent an expensive day at a trendy salon. Her hair was colored and styled and gobs of facial makeup were applied. When she returned home, she donned a full-length purple satin gown, a large gold medallion necklace, and silver spike heels. She called to me as she descended down the staircase, "Come see. How do I look?" I tried to hide my gape. How did she look? She looked like a seventy-five-year-old hooker! Her dress and necklace were hideous.

"You look great, Mom." How could I tell the truth? This woman spent $500 at the salon and probably twice that much on her wardrobe. The truth would have resulted in her cardiac arrest.

Lying is also necessary when raising children. Children are inherently curious beings who ask thousands of nosy questions, such as: Where do babies come from? Did you and Dad do it before you were married? Did you ever smoke pot? Were you ever arrested for mooning at a college frat party? Truthful answers to these type of questions often result in TOO MUCH INFORMATION! Thus, in such cases as these, lying is justifiable.

However, nowhere is lying more necessary than in marriage, unless divorce is the goal. There are certain truths that must go to the grave and need not be discussed with one's spouse. For example, a husband should never tell his wife that she is fat, wrinkled, nor old. Nor should he disclose that he'd rather go to the sports bar with his buddies, instead of the PTA carnival. A wife should never tell her husband that the best sex she ever had was with her college roommate. Nor should she admit to spending half the grocery budget on a designer purse. Lying is the best prevention for divorce.

In a perfect world, lying would not be necessary. We could readily admit to chopping down the proverbial cherry tree, frequenting a strip club, sleeping with the mailman, or working it out by hand. Unfortunately, in our imperfect world, lying is acceptable, justifiable, and mandatory. We must lie to save lives, to preserve our parent roles, and to survive our marriages. So the next time someone asks, "How old are you?" Thirty-nine is the only acceptable answer.

Compare and Contrast Paper

The compare and contrast paper is the examination of two or more things in order to establish their similarities and/or differences. This examination is used in daily lives to make choices between alternatives, such as which bottle of wine to purchase or which person to date. This is the **most** common type of essay assignment.

How to write Compare and Contrast

1. **First decide on two or more things to be examined**: *owning versus renting, political candidate platforms, before my high school reunion/after divorce.*

2. **Draft a topic sentence**: *The platforms of city council candidates, Bob Doowah and Sandra Smuck are similar and different.*

3. **Discuss the similarities**: *Opinions on neighborhood Block Watch, increased pay for police and fire protection, and garbage pick-up*

4. **Discuss the differences:** *Opinions on transportation services, public parks, and increased pay for city council members*

5. **Write a conclusion**.

How to write Compare *OR* Contrast

Often, things are only evaluated based on similarities **or** differences. For example, *There are several similarities between chicken livers and Rocky Mountain oysters.* In other evaluations, differences are the focal point, such as *My life drastically changed when I got divorced, or men's colds are worse than women's colds.* There are two ways to arrange compare or contrast papers.

1. **One side at a time** (This format is frequently used in before and after scenarios.)

    - Introduction with a topic sentence

    - Before my divorce or men's colds

- After my divorce or women's colds
- Conclusion

2. **Point-by-point** (This format is frequently used in making decisions.)

    - Introduction with a topic sentence: *When I moved from Youngstown, Ohio, to Phoenix, Arizona, I discovered many differences in the two cities. The weather, the employment opportunities, and the people were strikingly different.*
    - Discuss weather in Ohio vs. Arizona
    - Discuss employment in Ohio vs. Arizona
    - Discuss people in Ohio vs. Arizona *(Yes, there is a difference.* **Phoenix young men are adorable.) *(AT)**
    - Conclusion

Contrast Paper

The Interesting Lives of Mosquitoes

by Bugs R. Kuhl, PhD

OMG, it's summer time! For many parts of America, summer time is synonymous with mosquito time. According to entomological research, the critter responsible for the most human deaths world-wide is the pesky mosquito. Unlike humans, it is difficult to simply pull down the jeans and see the differences between boy and girl mosquitoes. However, there are significant differences between the mosquito sexes.

Though all mosquitoes have one pair of wings, six legs, and two eyes that allow them to see in multiple directions at once, boy mosquitoes are smaller than girl mosquitoes. Boy mosquitoes do not make the dreaded buzzing sound, and boy mosquitoes do not bite humans. Their proboscis is not ragged; thus, instead of chomping a blond woman wearing a black shirt, whom has recently eaten a banana, boys prefer to spend their ten to twenty days on earth drinking nectar from flowers and screwing girl mosquitoes.

In direct contrast, girl mosquitoes are femme fatales. These deadly ladies buzz in one's ear, delight in attacking children during a full moon, and thrive on sucking blood. Their serrated proboscis allows them the pleasure of siphoning blood from victims. Since a girl mosquito's life span can reach 100 days, her threat can last an entire summer. Further, the saliva of mosquitoes is said to contain some of the same ingredients found in rat poison.

Mosquitoes are the most dangerous critters on earth. Folks must beware of them--particularly the female ones. Like most female species on earth, girl mosquitoes live longer, talk a lot, and can suck anyone dry.

Cause and Effect Paper

A cause is an action, force, or influence that produces an effect. An effect is the result or product of a cause. *I had unprotected sex **(cause)** and got pregnant **(effect).*** When writing about the cause and effect relationship, the writer can reason in two ways: Effect-to-cause(s) or cause-to-effect(s).

Effect to Cause(s) Reasoning

This reasoning is better known as **Momma's reasoning**, for it answers the question why? Why'd you do dat? Why'd dat happen?

Effect = dropping out of college

- Why did he or she drop out of college? What caused him or her to drop out?
- List and explain the causes: ran out of money, got bored, found a decent job, moved to another state and went to work, etc.

Cause to Effect(s) Reasoning

This reasoning answers the questions: What are the results? What will happen if?

Cause = dropping out of college

- What are the results of dropping out? What will happen if one drops out of college?
- List and explain the effects: Did or will disappoint family and self, Did not or will not earn a degree, Did or will earn less money than those with degrees in particular work field, etc.

NOTE: Take any event, situation, or incident and reason either effect to causes or cause to effects, for example, a car accident. Why did the accident happen? (Effect to causes) **Or** what were the effects/results of the accident? (Cause to effects) Further, some essay questions ask for both causes and effects, e.g. What were the three major causes and three major effects of the American Civil War?

BEWARE: Faulty Reasoning Ahead

Sometimes an examination of the cause/effect relationship is flawed, and these flaws have fancy Latin names that we can't pronounce and have trouble spelling. Behold these flaws:

- My boy-toy and I had a tryst, and the earthquake hit. Our passion must have caused the earth to move.
- A black cat crossed in front of the oncoming car, and moments later the right tire blew. Damn those black cats.
- Because Julie had a goodnight's sleep, she aced her gynecological exam.
- **James is a fabulous football coach; he'll make a great high school principal.*(AT)**
- If we can build cars, we can stop terrorism.
- **Politicians engage in faulty reasoning on a routine basis. *(AT)**

Cause to Effect Paper

2 Is Better Than 1

by Mindy Merlot

"Don't hate me because I'm beautiful." I am. In my brief, twenty-five years of life, I have learned that I'm not going to earn a college degree, nor negotiate world peace. However, I have physical assets that could bring down the economy or any terrorist group with ease. However, since I had no prospects of solving those cumbersome issues, I decided to become a second wife. Within months of my decision, I found Edward, and my life surpassed Mach One, Eden, and Shangri-La!

Edward, a sixty-eight-year-old orthopedic surgeon with terminal heart disease, was of national renown. His first wife, Jessica, worked as a pharmacy store clerk while he was in medical school. Her earnings served to pay the rent on their tiny apartment and to buy groceries. After bearing and raising three children during their twenty-nine years of marriage, Jessica was out; two months later, I was in--both literally and figuratively. Edward gave me a huge, diamond ring that could choke a hippopotamus, and we flew on his time-shared, private jet to Reno. Within an hour after landing, we were married by a Nixon impersonator and drank champagne with the sleazy chapel staff. From that moment on, I was ecstatic. I was living the life I deserved.

Banished was my mundane life. I was finally treated as a princess. My former, 600-square-foot apartment became a palatial residence on the fifth fairway of the Dilly Dally Country Club. My tired, green sedan was replaced by a sleek, black convertible. A vast collection of designer clothes and accessories, purchased on weekend shopping binges to New York City or Rodeo Drive, jammed my closets. Several enhancement surgeries improved my outward, and I do mean outward, appearance. I had a personal trainer and weekly spa appointments; cleaning, meal preparation, and laundry duties were done by my Guatemalan housekeeper.

Further, unlike JoeyBob and Randy, my hometown boy-toys,

Edward was attentive. He scurried to open my car door, scampered to push the elevator button, and dashed to help me remove my leather jacket. He patted my heinie and stroked my arm as we dined at the by-invitation-only, upscale bistro party.

However, the best thing about Edward was that he could not afford to retire and keep me in the style to which I had easily become accustomed. He worked long hours during the week and was summoned to the hospital every other weekend. Thus, I had ample time to enjoy my various hobbies. I chaired the Heart Ball and spent hours addressing invitations, meeting with planners, and drinking mimosas with committee members. I volunteered at the rescue shelter for battered hamsters, and I took French lessons. My French tutor, Gaston, taught me all kinds of things about France and its culture, but I won't divulge the extent of his instruction for fear that Edward might read this.

When I became Edward's wife, my life changed. Gone were my days of poverty; I live in luxury. Before we were married, I made very sure that if Edward's heart gave out, I would be financially secure. Gaston was glad to have that information.

"Trés bien, Gaston!"

Process

Sometimes this arrangement is referred to as the Christmas Eve or Birthday Eve nightmare! Most folk have experienced the horror of buying an unassembled bicycle or new computer program. As they begin to read the assembly or download instructions, they query, "WTF?"

A process paper may be:

- Instructional or informational
- If it is instructional, do **not** write about something that you have **never** executed yourself. If you've never seduced your next door neighbor or stolen your parents' car when you were a teenager, you'll have difficulty persuading the reader that you are an expert. Choose a topic that you know how to execute. Further, your "how-to" instructions must be clearly understood by the reader at his/her **first** reading.
- If it is informational, such as how to embalm a body, you'll probably need to research the steps in the process.
- Usually organized chronologically--what happens first, second, etc.

How to write a process paper

1. **Draft a topic sentence.** For example, *Have you ever wanted to be a nerd but were afraid to try? You need only to have the right equipment and behave in the prescribed manner, and you, too, can be a nerd.*

2. **Next, clearly delineate the materials needed**. *To be a nerd, one would need: a pocket protector full of pens stuffed into a checkered shirt pocket, high-water black pants, black-rimmed glasses held together with white, adhesive tape.*

3. **Enumerate steps**. *Once you are dressed like a nerd, you are ready to act like a nerd in both the work place and social situations. At work you must... At a party you must...*

4. **Write a concluding statement.** *After you have the necessary attire and have mastered the appropriate behaviors in both the work place and social situations, anyone who meets you will know you are a nerd.*

Process Paper

This is an instructional process paper. Note the use of transitions to signal time: first, next, at last, finally, now, once, after.

Beer-Butt Chicken

by Momma Sipps

If you are at a loss as to what to serve at your next dinner party, consider making Beer-Butt Chicken. Your guests will be impressed by your culinary expertise, and those with a propensity for vulgarity will be duly entertained.

To make this delicious delicacy for eight people, you must first gather the necessary ingredients. You will need: two, whole chickens; two, 12-ounce cans of beer; a roll of un-waxed dental floss. In addition, you will need: one cup of brown sugar, paprika, one packet of dry taco seasoning, kosher salt and pepper. Preheat your barbeque grill to 350°. Remove the chickens' guts, wash the chickens, and pat them dry. Sit each chicken upright on its buttocks, and tie back the wings with dental floss.

Next, in a large mixing bowl, stir in the sugar, taco seasoning, and dashes of paprika, salt, and pepper. Once these ingredients are thoroughly mixed, liberally rub each bird with the seasonings. After each is sufficiently coated, open the beer and pour out three ounces from each can. Drink the six ounces as a reward.

Now shove the opened can of beer up the chicken's butt. Make sure the beer can remains upright. Spilling beer is worse than spilling beans. Carefully set the chicken in an aluminum pan. Place the upright birds on the grill over indirect heat, and roast for approximately two and one-half hours. Check frequently to ensure the grill temperature does not exceed 400°.

Use caution when removing the fowl from the grill. Gently lift them from their beer-can perches, and place them on a platter. Remove the beer and pans from the grill. Cut off the dental floss and carve the chickens.

Finally, as your guests sit down to dinner and devour your creation, you will be amazed by their accolades. After several bottles of wine, encourage them to rename your recipe in more graphic terms, such as Bud F#*ked Fowl.

Description Paper

A descriptive paper creates a clear, vivid, sensual picture for the reader. Thus, it relies heavily on the five senses: taste, smell, touch, hearing and sight. It is filled with details and can be organized spatially--top to bottom, left to right, far to near.

Using your five senses, evaluate this ramshackle. If you are a developer, can you convince your partners through an email that this house should be demolished? If you are heir to this property, can you convince your siblings that it is worth saving? If this is your grandparents' former home, can you describe your memories on the back porch, under the tree, or in the upstairs' bedroom?

How to write Description

1. **Determine the subject and write a topic sentence**: *Our family homestead should be donated to the Vernon Volunteer Fire Department.*

2. **Buy a thesaurus**. It abounds with sensual words and won't

bother your libido, nor the lack thereof.

3. **Use vivid words and examples to justify your position**: *The foul-smelling bat droppings on the second floor would have gagged a maggot.*

4. **Write a concluding statement.**

Description Paper

Growing Old Sucks

by Jack Schit

They are described as the golden years. The kids have graduated from college, are married, have children, and are ensconced in their lives. Now is the time for Grandma and Grandpa to enjoy their freedom from onerous responsibilities and relish their retirement. While many rejoice in this time of life, to put it bluntly, growing old sucks. In fact, growing old sucks from morning to bedtime.

At dawn, the urge to tinkle raises one from deep slumber. It doesn't matter how X-Rated the dream is, tinkling takes precedence. Now, not later. However, before accomplishing the bathroom task Grandma must first get out of bed. After fumbling across the nightstand for a pair of glasses and laboriously placing both feet on the floor, one calf seizes in a "charley horse." In excruciating pain, she limps to the bathroom. But before her butt hits the johnny seat, a sneeze erupts. Oops! Too late for the johnny! What a fabulous way to greet the day.

After a breakfast of bran flakes, the delightful fiber that tastes like styrofoam, Grandma and Grandpa plan their day. Last week, they'd been to the optometrist, the proctologist, the internist, and the podiatrist. They each had been declared healthy, or reasonably so, and were free to do whatever they chose today. Grandma wants to go to Bingo at the Italian Club. Grandpa wants to go hang out with his antique car collector friends. Since neither of them can drive at night, they sold their second car four years ago. How they rationalized that decision, one will never know. Now they must negotiate as to who takes the car and goes where.

The negotiation continues through a lunch of leftover spaghetti and watermelon--for fiber. Finally, they agree to go walk laps around the mall. When they enter the mall, Grandma decides she needs more substantial foundation-wear to hide her growing bulges. Grandpa stomps off to the bookstore as Grandma heads for the lingerie department. A saleslady insists that Grandma try on the newest invention for hiding unwanted cellulose. In the dressing room, as Grandma wiggles and jiggles to force her torso into the invention, she abruptly stops and stares in the full-length mirror. "Who are you?" she queries. "Who is that fat, old woman in the mirror?"

On the ride home from the mall, the couple is quiet. Grandma is wondering what happened to her body, and Grandpa is wondering what's for dinner. Dinner is from the market's freezer case--something that's supposed to taste like meatloaf, something that's meant to be mashed potatoes, and something short on apples and long on cinnamon. As the television news plays in the background, they indulge themselves with a glass of white zinfandel. Grandpa opines, "What the hell is going on in this country. Those damn Democrats will destroy us."

"Democrats?" counters Grandma. "It's the Republicans that got us into this mess. Don't you get it, you old fool? And to think I gave you one of my Democrat kidneys! You would have been dead without my kidney."

Grandpa grabs the TV remote control and switches channels to an old rerun, detective show. He meanders over to his recliner chair, props it back, nods off, and snores well above the high-volume, car-chase scene. Grandma ponders if the corns on her toes will stop throbbing. She pours another glass of wine. As she ambles toward their bedroom of forty-five years, she asks herself again, "What happened to my youth? What happened to the parties, the holiday dinners, the family vacations?"

The phone rings. "Hi, Mom. How are you? Listen; remember I told you I was writing a book? Well, I need your perspective. What sucks?"

"What sucks? I'll tell you what sucks. Your father sucks."

"Mom, that's way too much information for me."

"When you've lived as long as I have, you'll know all about the aging process. The so-called golden years are more like the song, *The Old Gray Mare She Ain't What She Used to Be.* When I open the refrigerator door, I can't remember whether I'm getting something out or putting something away. At least I still have my mind and can remember the names of my six grandchildren, 'Knock on wood.' Oops, I've got to go; someone is at the front door."

The Research Paper

When your college professor or employer asks you to write a research paper and your writing skills suck the big wazoo, you need to follow our advice. If you are tempted to pay someone else to write this paper or to steal a replica from the Internet, you suck! You are an idiot who paid good money for this book and are too stupid to realize that you are still stupid.

Buy, download, or borrow an English book that clearly delineates the research paper process. Our advice **merely summarizes** this task.

1. Gain an understanding of the assignment. Does the assignment ask you to discuss a process, to classify, to compare and/or to contrast, to persuade, to define, or to describe?

2. Pre-write until you can formulate one, clear, concise sentence, aka the **thesis statement.** This sentence is the road map or the force that controls the content of your paper. The following are examples:

    - *The Indian Removal Act of 1830 was one of the most infamous occurrences in the history of humanity.*
    - *The proposal of C. Deucethem and Howe is far superior to the proposals submitted by Jordan Landfill and Naughty Potty, LLC.*
    - *The use of therapy dogs in hospitals improves both the physical and the psychological health of patients.*

3. Gather facts, statistics, and other information to support your thesis statement. Gone are the days of copying your essay from your parents' encyclopedia. You cannot write a quality research paper in ONE day. You must:

    - Get off your fat behind, and go to the library.
    - Use the Internet to search and retrieve information.
    - Know the differences between good and bad, hard and soft, and primary and secondary evidence.

GOOD	**BAD**
Scholarly journals	Popular magazines
Reference magazines	Tabloids
	On-line resources that can be edited

HARD	**SOFT**
Facts and statistics	Interpretations of data

PRIMARY	**SECONDARY**
Eyewitness accounts and/ or photos	Interpretations of events
Original literary works	Book reviews
Speeches	Editorials
Historical documents	Biographies

- Scrutinize your sources to be sure they are credible and accurate. Always check the source(s) publication date. With rapid technological and scientific discoveries, facts change.

4. Keep an accurate accounting of all sources, for you will need to document sources in the bibliography or "Works Cited" section of the paper. (If your professor dictates the citation style to be used, e.g. MLA, Chicago, or APA, use the Internet to help with formatting. We could explain each of these styles, but you only need to know which one you're **required** to use. After all, this style competition is educational bull s%#t.)

5. When you are ready to write your paper, arrange your thoughts chronologically, logically, or from least to most important.

6. **Never** copy word-for-word from a source unless you use quotation marks and appropriately credit the original author. *"There is no such thing as a brain fart; it is cranial flatulence."* (Creighton, 2008). If you choose to summarize or paraphrase a source, appropriately credit the author. *In her study of East Tennessee dialect, Creighton found no difference in the pronunciation of all and oil.* (2008).

You Suck Uh-Oh!

Failure to give credit to the original author is plagiarism--a fancy word for stealing.

7. After writing your paper, seek assistance from the college writing center, English teachers, and/or literate peers. Revise, revise, revise.

An example of a research paper, written in APA style, follows on the next page. This is purely fictitious, so do not copy nor quote any of the information.

The Origin of the Toilet

Many people take their indoor, water-conserving, chocolate-colored or red toilet for granted. They can only recall the days of the white, porcelain pot and are delighted that potties now come in custom colors with a variety of seats to satisfy any fantasy. However, research indicates that the evolution of the modern toilet spanned centuries.

In 202 B.C., the Han dynasty ruled China, and culture was elevated to new heights (Wright, 2004). After the second birthday of his son, I. Flingpoo, the Emperor held a summit. According to Han historian, Wright (2004), I. Fling suffered from an affliction that caused him to relieve himself in the Royal Gardens of Naaki and to attempt to toss his deposits over the Great Wall. In his address to the summit of inventors, the Emperor stated:

> The Empress and I are forever grateful that you are gathered here today. The troops of General Tse Tse Fli are complaining about the odors of the palace. Thus, we fear our dear son and heir to the throne, I. Fling, is in need of recreation. His current interest should be redirected to create a proper dumping ground for his talents. Expedience is a must. The first man to bring me a new device will live in luxury for the rest of his life. (p. 231)

Six months after the summit, several inventors responded. One had designed an apparatus resembling a modern-day sling shot; another offered a bead and string contraption for counting; a third presented a cumbersome, wood box. Research by Sunny and Char (2007) indicated that the Emperor was intrigued with the wooden box, faced with clear, glass screen. Its creator, X. Boxfu, demonstrated how a small, white ball could be batted back and forth across the screen. However, none of these devices proved effective. I. Fling became the Emperor in 170 B.C. and continued to decorate the neighborhood. (p. 167)

For the next 1,500 years, little attention was paid to bathrooming habits. Historian, Mia Angst (2004) , noted, “People just liked doing it in the streets. They subscribed to the notion, ‘When you’ve got to go, you've got to go,' regardless of the locale." (p. 41) As a result, disease was widespread, and some researchers estimate that over one million people died for lack of proper human waste disposal. (Charmain & Softones, 1995)

By 1798, the death toll due to human pees and poops had climbed to four million. In America, people demanded that the government solve this pandemic. An unknown writer for the *Marblehead Mast* penned a scathing editorial:

> Hey, dudes. Wake up! We're a new country fraught with problems, and wallowing in feces shouldn't be one of them. It is urgent that Congress stop slinging bulls*#t and deal with it. If you fail to do it now, this will go on for another 300 years! By 2010, our heirs will be buried in piles of crap from which they will be unable to extricate themselves. Listen to distinguished Senator Sean O'Connor of Massachusetts, "Pahty should not take precedence over potty." (p. 3)

Despite the public outcry for intervention, the problem of proper human waste disposal continued. The Congress maintained it was a state problem; each state maintained it was a local problem. Thus, across America, municipalities, villages, and towns were faced with regulating "number 1" and "number 2". For example, Latimer City Council in Alabama passed an ordinance that read in part: "Any person seen peeing on a tree or pooping in the grass will be subject to a $100 fine." (Sunny & Char, p. 69) Jefferson, Oregon, Village Trustees declared: "If you alleviate yourself in the backyard, wrap it up in newspaper, and throw it in the trash can. Failure to do so, may result in a fine." (Sunny & Char, p. 71) In Holbrook, Iowa, the voters approved this change to the town charter: "Human waste shall be dealt with accordingly: (a) dig a deep hole in the ground, do your business over the hole. When you are done, toss several shovels of dirt on top of it; (b) if you do not have a job, beat your wife, nor have any good reason to stick around, drop yourself into a deep hole and get a friend to bury you." (Sunny & Char, p.82)

A number of distinguished women, led by schoolmarm, Rebeckah Johnson, convinced the mayor of Gopher Flats, West Virginia, that it was grossly inappropriate to see individuals squatting over earthen holes in their backyards. Johnson argued, " Young, impressionable minds should not witness such events while walking to and from school." In 1870,

Mayor Boog Cates agreed and ordered that all holes had to be encased with a wooden structure. He signed unprecedented legislation that was known familiarly as the "Outhouse" law. (Fiddlefarts, 1912)

Then, in 1892, Ian and Ida Haddit left Scotland and came to the United States in search of a better life. While some historians noted that Haddit would have been satisfied to rent a New York City apartment, Ida convinced him to board a train and travel to Ashtabula, Ohio. (Fiddlefarts, p.17) In her diary, she wrote:

> Ian is dismayed that I insisted we move to Ashtabula, Indian words for "river of many fishes." However, I read the true account of the origin of the word, Ashtabula. Seems the Indian chief had an old wife named, Bulah. Then he took another gorgeous, young girl named Roxy. Throughout the remainder of the chief's life, he slept with his ass-to-Bulah. Sounds like my kind of place! (Haddit, p.5)

Once Ian and Ida had settled into their environs on the Lake Erie shore, he became the verbal punching bag of the Finnish and Italian immigrants with whom he worked. These dock workers, described as "hooligans" and "Satan's offspring," taunted Ian by denouncing Scotland as England's bastard child and by mispronouncing his name as Eye Am Going To.... (Zamboni, 1986) So with the permission of Ida, Ian anglicized his named to John. Most researchers posit that the Ian-to-John change led Haddit to reconsider his vocation. (Charmain and Softones, p.452)

For the next three years, Haddit designed and tinkered. He sawed; he hammered; he welded; he dug, and tested. However, each of his creations failed. His meager savings account was nearly empty, forcing Ida to take in laundry and mending for wealthy, dock owners. "The cruelty of failure and of poverty compelled him to try one more time." He labored fourteen hours a day for two weeks, and on July 21, 1898, his apparatus was tested. Haddit sat down on the porcelain, emptied his bowels, wiped himself with a page from last year's catalog, reached above his head, and yanked the chain. (Charmain & Softones, p.560) According to a July 23 newspaper interview, Haddit, stated: "I was stunned! I was expecting to be covered again with spewing manure, but instead of going up, it went down! It went down. Down the pipe, down the pipe, and emptied into an underground tank. I did it!" When queried as to the name of his invention, Haddit replied, “John.” (*Bula Blows,* p.6)

During the Victorian Era, Haddit’s invention was renamed. Some historians have suggested that staid, proper, Victorian women found “John” to be offensive and preferred a more gentile term, “water closet.” During the next century, Haddit’s product underwent a number of changes. Cities built expansive sewer systems to accommodate the demand for waste removal. Eventually, rural outhouses became an artifact of the past. (Sunny & Char, p. 926)

The evolution of the modern toilet spanned centuries from the Han dynasty in 202 B.C. to a Lake Erie port in 1898. Though most historians credit John Haddit as the inventor, the dedication, determination, and perseverance of thousands made the toilet a reality. Without the combined efforts of these multitudes, the environmental sustainability of America would have been seriously compromised.

References

Angst, M. (2004). *Sewage in the streets: What a mess.* Boston: O' Leary and Sons.

Haddit Scores. [Interview with J. Haddit] (1898, July 23). *Bula Blows,* p. 6.

Charmain, U., & Softones, I. (1995). *The disposal of human waste.* New York: Randy Press.

Fiddlefarts, F. (1912). *Interesting facts of the 19th century.* Beech Springs: Mount Printing.

Haddit, I. (1892). *Personal diary entry.*

Government Must Act. (1799, August 12). *Marblehead Mast,* p. 3.

Sunny, S., & Char, E. (2007) *The history of bathrooming.* Dorset: Sandy University Press.

Wright, E. (2004). *Contributions of the han dynasty to modern society.* Orwell: Rock Creek Publishing.

Zamboni, Z. (1986) *A question of tolerance: The shipping industry nightmares.* Harbor: Lake College for Erie Women Press.

Revising Strategies

We are well aware that this picture is crude and disgusting, but we must have your full attention as we near the end of the writing section.

Ernest Hemingway once said, "The first draft of anything is shit." If you forget to revise, your writing will not only suck, it will be crap! Great writing is the result of rewriting, revising, and massaging--a foreign concept in an instant-messaging world. Hello, you are not perfect, nor is Bitsy Blondell. Remember this awful paragraph? Bitsy needs to revise it.

Dogs and Me

by Bitsy Blondell

Dogs are great companions for single women. How do I know that? My life sucks! If I had a dog, I'd have companionship. Dogs are friends. My dog would love me. Even though my boss hates me and will not promote me. My dog would replace my friends. My friends party too much and releve their high school days. Not to mention all those dumb boys that ask me out once and never call again!! If I had a dog, I would be soo happy. Just a little dog. I wouldn't even mind cleaning up pee on the carpet. Dogs are single women's best friends. If I can't get a dog, I'll get a kitten.

Let the revisions begin!

1. **Vary sentences.** Adults don't talk babytalk. When adults write babytalk sentences, their writing sucks! Look at Bitsy's sentences.

- Dogs are friends.

- My dog would love me.

The use of more complex and longer sentences indicates not only adulthood, but also intelligence and sophistication. Bitsy's sentences might be rewritten as:

- Regardless of their size, dogs are loyal and protective of their owner.

- **Dogs are better than children: dogs don't talk back, beg for a ride to the mall, nor borrow money for a night at the movies.*(AT)**

2. **Use specific words**, such as lively adjectives, vivid verbs, and words that relate to the five senses. An on-line or hard copy Thesaurus can help identify descriptive words.

- I want a dog. (Boring)

- I want a registered, black, miniature poodle puppy. (Specific)

- Bitsy lives in an apartment. (Boring)

- Bitsy's gloomy, one-bedroom, apartment on the corner of Elm and Ash had deteriorated into a ruin of cracked windows, peeling paint, and termite-infested lumber. (Specific)

- Bitsy said she'd be back later. (Instead of "said," try: spoke, whispered, mumbled, cried, yelled, sobbed, screamed. These are vivid verbs.)

- The annoying, intercom buzzer was whirring in Bitsy's ear. (sense of hearing)

- Bitsy's apartment reeked of stale beer, gardenia perfume, and dog pee. (sense of smell)

3. Use transitions to help the reader follow the writer's thoughts. Transitions are words and phrases that show logical connections and relationships between ideas. Transitions send signals to the reader about time, place, examples, conclusions, comparisons and contrasts. Below are given some common transitions:

first	next	since	beyond
second (ly)	soon	in retrospect	to the left
third (ly)	until	in summary	above
last (ly)	similarly	in conclusion	to the right
finally	in contrast	thus	opposite
in conclusion	on one hand	therefore	because
after (wards)	on the other hand	as mentioned earlier	as previously stated
again	although	below	in fact
such as	for example	specifically	in spite of
nevertheless	however	on the contrary	in short

4. Organize ideas to convince the reader that the writer is knowledgeable. Bitsy's thoughts are scattered and hard to follow. She attempts to convince us she wants a dog, and then out of NOWHERE says she'll settle for a kitten! Bitsy is crazy. What sane person would want to cope with a litter box, fur balls, and claws?

5. Use technology, such as "spell check" or "grammar check," available in most word processing programs. Bitsy forgot to do so.

- Misspelled *"relive"* and *"so"*
- Overused the exclamation mark
- Wrote sentence fragments: *Even though my boss hates me and*

will not promote me. Not to mention all those dumb boys that ask me out once and never call again!!

6. Read your writing aloud., Does it make sense? Does it wander aimlessly? Is your precise opinion clear? Have **at least** one other person read it. Another pair of eyes usually can spot errors and omissions. Finally, try reading your paper backwards. If it is well-organized, it should be just as clear as when you read it forward.

Since we royally trashed Bitsy's paragraph, she asked for the opportunity to rewrite it. Behold her final endeavor:

Dogs and Me

by Bitsy Blondell

Dogs are great companions for single women. I came to understand that when I moved from my small, Arkansas hometown to New York City to study acting. When I first moved in to my tiny, dark, one-room apartment, I wondered why there were so many inside locks on the door. Of course, after the third break-in to my hovel, I got the message. Thus, I made the decision to get a dog, not only for protection, but also to add some vitality to my boring life as a student and waitress at Juang's Pizzeria. After visiting several animal shelters without success, old, mean Juang said his registered, miniature black poodle had been diddled by some mangy stray and was due to have pups any day. If I could wait six weeks, Juang would give me one of his so-called disgusting mutts. Seven weeks later, I was holding an adorable black and brown stoodle (half stray; half poodle), whom I named Sadie. Over the next year, Sadie grew to twenty pounds and became the guardian of our property. Even the apartment house manager is afraid to enter our home unless I have Sadie on a leash. Sadie has revitalized my mundane existence. She makes me walk through Central Park and window shop along Fifth Avenue. She snuggles against me as we watch our previously-recorded soap operas, and she sleeps at my head every night. Further, she seems to delight in my impersonations of classic actresses, like Helga Hosendorf and Brandy O' Doome. Sadie has brought security and joy to my life as a single, up-and-coming star in *The Secret Opening of Jenna the Nymph.*

Things that Drive Us Nuckin' Futs

Momma was in the kitchen preparing Beer-Butt chicken. Six-year-old Kayla was reading a book her baby brother. "Look at the picture, Tommy. It's a frickin' flower. It's a frickin' violet."

Momma knocked over the chicken, and beer splattered across the counter. She rushed into the playroom and demanded, "Kayla! What did you say?"

"Look at this, Momma. *A frickin violet!*"

African Violet

Things that Drive Us Nuckin' Futs

Poor speech and stupid spelling make us crazy! We do not give a beaver's butt crack about your geographic locale, nor do we care if you heard it or saw it in the media. If you make these mistakes, you're ignorant and you suck.

- irregardless (NOT a word; regardless is a word.)
- ain't or tain't (Correct form: am not, is not, are not)
- Where are you at? (Correct form: Where are you?)

- I'm fixin' to go to the plastic surgeon. (Really? What are you going to get fixed?)
- She can't hardly wait to cram her body into spandex and go to the gym. (Correct form: She can't wait to cram her body into spandex and go to the gym.)
- If flying be safe, why do I have to go to the airport terminal? (Correct form: If flying is safe, why do I have to go to the airport terminal?)
- yens and yous (Correct form: you. We don't care if you're from Pittsburgh!)
- ain't got no (Correct form: do not have)
- These ones are mine. (Correct form: These are mine. These boxers are mine.)
- Your dog is pretty ugly. (Uh-oh, and to think you spent all that money on a mutt.)
- Betcha Noah wished he had kilt them two mosquitoes. (Correct form: I bet Noah wished that he had killed those two mosquitoes.

Please excuse Dan from school yesterday.
He had the dir diarh diare.
He had the shits.
Mrs. Smith

The above is a replication of an actual note delivered to an elementary school teacher. Diarrhea comes from the Greek word that means to flow through and is one of the most misspelled words in English. So when in doubt as how to spell a word correctly, look in the dictionary, get the computer to spell it, or choose other words that have similar meaning. Most folk understand such phrases as the shits, loose bowels, or locked bowel in the open position.

These are some of our favorite misspelled words that have left us convulsed in laughter because we know the writers are dingleberries:

- Youthinasia is a serious problem. (I agree overpopulation is a problem in the Orient, but you meant to write euthanasia.)
- The valleyvictorian strutted across the stage and high-fived her principal. (Was the writer describing a character from a Dickens' novel? No, the valedictorian.)
- youraneight. (How many times do I have to take the drug test until I score a 10? Urinate is the correct spelling.)
- Timbuckedtwo. (That Tim must be a stud, but the correct spelling is Timbuktu.)

Prescription Practice

englishdoesntsuck.com
123 Easy Street, Bumblebee Trail, AZ 86079

Name: You, Dumb A$$
Date: Today
Address: Wherever you hang

Rx: Until your writing improves, complete the practice section.

Alice Courtney, M.Ed. and Sue Skidmore, Ed.D.
Dispense as written. Substitution not permissible.

Yep, this script's for you. If you want to be a competent writer, you must practice. On the following pages are ribald, raucous practices for your entertainment. If you choose to do them, you will laugh and learn. Remember what Woody Allen said, "I'm really good at sex because I practice a lot alone." Suck it up! Practice.

Practice: The Sentence

The following may be complete sentences, fragments, or run-ons. Indicate C for complete; F for fragment; GAS for green-apple squits.

1. _____ Upon Jack's return from his undercover drug surveillance assignment in Mexico.

2. _____ Why would anyone elect to have enhancement surgery?

3. _____ The dog strolled onto the neighbor's front lawn and he took a big doo on her sidewalk and whizzed on her rose bushes.

4. _____ Someone once said that women should marry archaeologists; they continue to love their old wives.

5. _____ Wear *Depends*® to the football games you won't miss a play.

6. _____ With the storm causing the plane to rock from side to side.

7. _____ Phoenix, Arizona, a city filled with aguaholics.

Answers

1. F Upon Jack's return from his undercover drug surveillance assignment in Mexico, **he vowed to never drink tequila again.**

2. C

3. GAS The dog strolled onto the neighbor's front lawn, and he took a big doo on her sidewalk, and whizzed on her rose bushes. **(Comma before and)**

4. C

5. GAS Wear *Depends*® to the football game**, and** you won't miss a play. (**Add comma + and) OR** Wear *Depends*®to the football game; you won't miss a play. (**; between game/you)**

6. F With the storm causing the plane to rock from side to side, **many passengers were searching for their barf bags.**

7. F **Phoenix, Arizona, is a city filled with aguaholics.*(AT)** One can easily die from the lack of liquid refreshment.

Practice: Punctuation Marks

The following are either correct as written or are in need of punctuation:

comma	semi-colon	exclamation point	apostrophe
colon	period	quotation marks	hyphen

1. Most men should keep their zippers in the upright and locked position unless they want to advertise
2. When the teacher in Dallas Texas showed a picture of a garden hoe to the class one child offered My sister's a ho and she doesn't look like that.
3. The boys called Virginia my best friend in high school Virgin for short but not for long.
4. The following is a favorite adage of Iowans Hooray Hooray Its the first of May. Outdoor f@#king begins today
5. To douche or not to douche that is the question is a famous quote by Trish Brown.
6. Upon my brothers engagement my grandmother told us if he can sleep with that woman we can eat with her.
7. The following should be avoided rattlesnakes scorpions and Black Widow spiders.
8. After the smoke cleared, one could easily see that the hamburgers were not edible.
9. Theyre going to the football game tonight and theyre bringing tube steaks.
10. Hey When are we going to get our navels pierced.
11. When she spied her brother in law in his tightie whities she remarked Its a small world after all.

12. Tom went to the car wash and then he discovered that hed left his credit card at the Not-Tell Hotel.

13. I like coffee I like tea I like girls and the girls like me.

14. Lets go to West Virgina for the summer there are no lifeguards in the gene pool.

15. Middle-aged men shouldn't wear Speedos®.

16. Due to inclement weather, our plane was delayed. Thus, we spent most of our time browsing the high-priced shops in the airport.

Answers

1. Correct

2. When the teacher in Dallas, Texas, showed a picture of a garden hoe to the class, one child offered, " My sister's a ho, and she doesn't look like that."

3. The boys called Virginia, my best friend in high school, "Virgin" for short, but not for long.

4. The following is a favorite adage of Iowans: Hooray! Hooray ! It's the first of May. Outdoor f@#king begins today!

5. "To douche or not to douche that is the question," is a famous quote by Trish Brown.

6. Upon my brother's engagement, my grandmother told us, "If he can sleep with that woman, we can eat with her."

7. The following should be avoided: rattlesnakes, scorpions, and Black Widow spiders.

8. Correct

9. They're going to the football game tonight, and they're bringing tube steaks.

10. Hey! When are we going to get our navels pierced?

11. When she spied her brother-in-law in his tightie whities, she remarked, "It's a small world after all."

12. Tom went to the car wash, and then he discovered that he'd left his credit card at the Not-Tell Hotel.

13. I like coffee, I like tea, I like girls, and the girls like me.

14. Let's go to West Virginia for the summer; there are no lifeguards in the gene pool.

15. and 16. Correct

Practice: Agreement

Choose the correct verb form.

1. Tattoos and piercings in outrageous places astounds/astound even young people.
2. Either James or Julia was/were scheduled to volunteer at the Condom Crisis Center today.
3. The male dance group, STUDS, performs/perform nightly at Aunt Fanny's Salon.
4. The grove of aspen trees is/are alive with killer bees.
5. Scandal is the main staple that sell/sells trash newspapers.
6. One hundred years has/have gone by since acne was discovered, yet no cures has/have been found.
7. A bottle of wine, a loaf of sourdough bread, and a hunk makes/make the perfect afternoon delight.
8. **Why is/are no one outraged when women wear/wears men's boxers and t-shirts? Yet everyone is/are stunned when men wear/wears women's underwear.*(AT)**

Answers

1. astound
2. was
3. performs
4. is
5. sells
6. years have, cures have
7. make
8. is, wear, is, wear

If necessary correct the following sentences to make pronouns agree in number or person with the nouns to which they refer.

1. The dog strolled onto the neighbor's property and doo-dooed in her/their yard.

2. Some universities require its/their professors to be finger-printed and undergo background checks.

3. If everybody is going to drink margaritas tonight, he or she/they better have a designated driver.

4. The teenager is a curious sort; he or she/they sleep all day and roam all night.

5. As I was adding olive juice to the martini, I spilled it/ the olive juice on the bar.

6. My parents are gamblers, but I hate it/gambling.

7. **Dogs are better than children; they/dogs don't whine, beg for a ride to the mall, or run up massive credit card bills. *(AT)**

Answers

1. her
2. their
3. he or she
4. he or she
5. the olive juice
6. gambling
7. dogs

Practice: Split Infinitives, Dangling Participles, Misplaced Modifiers, and Faulty Parallelism

The following are either correct as written or in need of revision:

1. Except when pickled, I don't like cauliflower.
2. Industrial engineers are highly trained, creative, and have a knowledge of ergonomics.
3. The boy went careening down the driveway just as we arrived in a grocery cart.
4. After playing poker on the Internet all evening, the dirty dishes were still on the kitchen table.
5. The yenta likes to incessantly talk about the match-making she's done.
6. While driving home from the football game, two fans were brawling in the middle of the street.
7. I overheard a braggart say, " Mine is three inches wide and seven inches in length."
8. Teenagers prefer texting, twitting, and to shop at high-end malls.
9. My grandfather came to live with us at the age of six.
10. I wanted to quickly finish the steamy novel before my engine overheated.

Answers

1. I don't like cauliflower unless it's pickled.
2. Industrial engineers are highly trained, creative, and ergonomically proficient.
3. Just as we arrived, the boy went careening down the driveway in a grocery cart.

4. The dirty dishes were still on the kitchen table because I'd played poker on the Internet all evening.

5. The yenta likes to talk incessantly about the match-making she's done.

6. While driving home from the football game, I saw two fans brawling in the middle of the street.

7. I overheard a braggart say, "Mine is three inches wide and seven inches long."

8. **Teenagers prefer texting, twitting, and shopping at high-end malls.*(AT)**

9. When I was six-years-old, my grandfather came to live with us.

10. I wanted to finish quickly the steamy novel before my engine overheated.

Practice: Goof Ball Spelling

1. The best advice/advise I ever received was to never leave home in dirty underwear/underwhere.

2. **The elicit/illicit behavior of the Congressman affected/effected the outcome of the election.*(AT)**

3. She had to/too much to/too drink and past/passed out on the dance floor.

4. Do you have a hole/whole in your head? Can't you here/hear me? Are/our you stupid or just a dirt bag?

5. Rather than/then go to the bordello, James chose to stay at home and play pocket pool.

Answers

1. advice, underwear

2. illicit, affected

3. too, to, passed

4. hole, hear, are

5. than

Practice: Sins 6 and 7

The salaries paid to American coaches and athletes are outrageous. Willy Score, football coach at Forsaken State University, will make four million dollars in the 2010 season. It won't matter if he wins or looses, due to the fact that he has a three-year contract. He will still take home the money. Irv Irons can lie down his golf clubs and earn over $100 million in endorsements. Even Roach Kawalski who played bad in the World Basketball Championship games earns in the neighborhood of $40 million. Latimer Lions' pitcher, Buzzy Oph, recently signed a ten-year deal worth $275 million!!! These salaries are outrageous, and you should just not go to sporting events.

Correct Edit

The salaries paid to American coaches and athletes are outrageous. Willy Score, football coach at Forsaken State University, will make **$4 million** in the 2010 season. It **will not** matter if he wins or **loses because** he has a three-year contract. He will still **bring** home the money. Irv Irons can **lay** down his golf clubs and earn over $100 million in endorsements. Even Roach Kawalski who played **badly** in the World Basketball Championship games earns in the neighborhood of $40 million. Latimer Lions' pitcher, Buzzy Oph, recently signed a ten-year deal worth $275 million**!** These salaries are outrageous, and **no one should go to** sporting events.

Acknowledgements

Acknowledgements

A number of dedicated people were instrumental in guiding us through this endeavor. We appreciate the generosity of Randy Bronner, our banking advisor and Greg Podd, our accounting guru. We are grateful for the work of our artists, Don Pedersen and Kolby McLean for bringing our words to illustration. Our editors, Bobbi Fisher and Jen Jeras Galanis, provided immeasurable support and humor throughout this journey. Without their technological expertise, we would have floundered.

Further, we thank Principal Arnholt for his mentoring and our favorite Happy Hour establishment, Z Tejas, for quenching our thirst.

"True, I can survive without it, but it's much more fun with it."

Appendix

Paragraph Format

Topic Sentence: ____

____

Supporting Evidence 1: ______________________________________

____

____

Details: ____

____

____

Supporting Evidence 2: ______________________________________

____

____

Details: ____

____

____

Supporting Evidence 3: ______________________________________

____

____

Details: ____

____

____

Closing: ____

____

Essay Format

Introduction and Thesis Statement: ______________________________

____

____

Body Paragraph 1
Topic Sentence: ____

____

Supporting Evidence: ____

____

____

Details: ____

____

____

Body Paragraph 2
Topic Sentence: ____

____

Supporting Evidence: ____

____

____

Details: ____

____

____

Body Paragraph 3
Topic Sentence: ____

____

Supporting Evidence: ____

____

____

Details: ____

____

____

Conclusion and restatement of thesis: ____________________________

____

____

Index

Index

Desiree? Desiree?

Ooops!

Made in the USA
Lexington, KY
29 May 2010